CAUSE TO HIDE

(AN AVERY BLACK MYSTERY—BOOK 3)

BLAKE PIERCE

BOOKS BY BLAKE PIERCE

RILEY PAIGE MYSTERY SERIES
ONCE GONE (Book #1)
ONCE TAKEN (Book #2)
ONCE CRAVED (Book #3)
ONCE LURED (Book #4)
ONCE HUNTED (Book #5)
ONCE PINED (Book #6)
ONCE FORSAKEN (Book #7)

MACKENZIE WHITE MYSTERY SERIES
BEFORE HE KILLS (Book #1)
BEFORE HE SEES (Book #2)
BEFORE HE COVETS (Book #3)
BEFORE HE TAKES (Book #4)

AVERY BLACK MYSTERY SERIES
CAUSE TO KILL (Book #1)
CAUSE TO RUN (Book #2)
CAUSE TO HIDE (Book #3)
CAUSE TO FEAR (Book #4)

KERI LOCKE MYSTERY SERIES
A TRACE OF DEATH (Book #1)
A TRACE OF MURDER (Book #2)

PROLOGUE

When he made his way out across the vacant lot, dawn was burning off the last of the night. The slightest bit of rain had fallen the night before, creating a mist of fog that crept along the ground. He walked slowly, methodically, as if he did this every morning.

To all sides were the foundations of houses—houses that would never be finished. He supposed the frames had gone up five or six years ago, only to be left abandoned when the housing crisis hit. For some reason, it enraged him. So much promise for a family and a builder, only to end up failing miserably in the end.

Against the fog, he looked gaunt—tall and thin, like a living scarecrow. His black overcoat blended perfectly with the light gray wisps. It was an ethereal scene. It made him feel ghostlike. It made him feel legendary, nearly invincible. He felt as if he were a part of the world and it, a part of him.

But there was nothing natural about his presence there. In fact, he had been planning this for weeks. Months, really. The years that had come before had really just ushered him along, pushing him toward this moment.

He walked through the fog and listened to the city. The hustle and bustle lay perhaps a mile away. He was in a forgotten part of town, decrepit, a part of town that had suffered economic collapse. So many dead hopes and dreams littered the fog-strewn ground.

It all made him want to burn.

Patiently, he waited. He paced back and forth with no real purpose. He walked along the edge of the empty street and then into the construction area among the skeletons of houses that never were. He stalked about, waiting for another figure to show itself in the fog. Knowing that the universe would send it to him.

Finally, it appeared.

Even before the figure came fully into view, he could sense it through dawn's weak light and the slithering fog. The figure was feminine.

This was what he had waited for. Destiny was being knitted together right before him.

With his heart thundering in his chest, he stepped forward, doing his best to seem natural and calm. He opened his mouth and started to call for a dog that was not there. In the fog, his voice did not sound like his own; it was thin and wavering, like a phantom.

He reached into the pocket of his long coat and withdrew a retractable dog leash that he had purchased the day before.

1

"Sweet Pea!" he called out.

It was the sort of name that would confuse a passerby before they had time to really even give him a second glance.

"Sweet Pea!"

The figure of the woman came closer, stepping through the fog. He saw that she had her own dog, taking it for its morning walk. It was one of those small pretentious dogs, the sort that looked more like a rat. Of course, he knew this about her. He knew just about everything about her morning schedule.

"Everything okay?" the woman asked.

He could see her face now. She was much younger than he was. Twenty years, at least.

He held up the empty leash and gave the woman a sad sort of smile. "My dog got loose. I'm pretty sure she came this way, but I don't hear her."

"Oh no," the woman said.

"Sweet Pea!" he yelled again.

At the woman's feet, her little dog lifted its leg and peed. The woman barely seemed to notice. She was looking at him now. Something very close to recognition filled her eyes. She tilted her head. An uncertain smile touched the corners of her mouth. She took a tiny step backward.

He reached into his other coat pocket and wrapped his hand around the handle of the hammer he had hidden there. He brought it out with a speed that surprised even him.

He struck her hard on top of the head with it. The sound it made in the quiet lot, in the blanket of fog, was almost nothing. *Thunk.*

Her eyes went glassy. When she collapsed to the ground, the traces of that small smile were still at the corners of her mouth.

Her little dog sniffed at her and then looked up to him. It gave a pathetic little bark. He stepped toward it and growled lightly. The dog peed a little more, backed away, and then went running out of the lot, its leash dragging behind it.

He pocketed the hammer and the useless leash. He then looked down at her body for a moment and slowly reached for it, the only sound left that of the dog's barking, echoing endlessly in the rolling fog of morning.

CHAPTER ONE

Avery sat the last of the boxes down on the floor of her daughter's new apartment and felt like crying. The moving truck had pulled away from the curb downstairs five minutes ago and there was no going back now: Rose had an apartment of her own. Avery felt the pit growing in her stomach; this was completely different than her living in a college dorm, where there were friends at every corner and the security of the campus police.

Rose would be living alone now. And Avery still hadn't accepted it. A very short time ago, Rose had been endangered because of Avery's last case—and that was something that Avery still harbored massive guilt over. To have Rose now out on her own after such an ordeal felt irresponsible on Avery's part. It made her feel like a failure as a mother. It also made her very scared for her daughter. And that was saying something, coming from a decorated Homicide detective.

She's eighteen, Avery thought. *You can't hold onto her forever, especially when your grip on her was loose, if not non-existent, during her formative years.*

How had Rose grown up so fast? How had she become such a beautiful, independent, and driven woman? Avery certainly couldn't take credit for it, as she had been absent for most of Rose's life.

All that aside, it made her feel proud to watch her daughter as she unpacked her own dishes and placed them into her own cupboards. Despite the tumultuous childhood and teen years she had faced, Rose had made it. The future was hers for the taking, and it started with putting her Dollar Store dishes into the cupboards of her first apartment.

"I'm proud of you, kid," Avery said. She made her way through the maze of boxes that occupied the floor of Rose's living room.

"For what?" Rose said.

"Surviving," Avery said with a laugh. "I know I didn't necessarily make it easy on you."

"You didn't. But Dad did okay. And that's not a dig against you."

Avery felt a pang of sorrow.

"I know."

Avery knew that such an admission was hard for Rose. Avery knew that her daughter was still trying to figure out the footing of their relationship. For a typical estranged mother and daughter, reconciliation was hard enough. But they had both been through hell lately. From Rose being stalked by a serial killer and moved to a safe house, to the post-traumatic stress disorder Avery was wrestling with from running to Rose's rescue, there were mountain-sized obstacles to get over. And even something as simple as moving boxes into her daughter's new apartment was a huge step along the way of repairing the relationship Avery so badly wanted with her.

Taking that step required some sort of normalcy—a normalcy that wasn't always available in the world of a work-obsessed detective.

She joined Rose in the kitchen and helped her unpack the boxes labeled KITCHEN. As they worked together to unpack them, Avery felt herself close to tears again.

What the hell? When have I ever gotten this emotional?

"Do you think you'll be okay?" Avery asked, doing what she could to keep conversation going. "This isn't like a college dorm. You're legitimately on your own. Are you ready for that after…well, after everything you've been through?"

"Yes, Mom. I'm not a little girl anymore."

"Well, that's very clear."

"Besides," she said, putting the last dish away and setting the empty box aside. "I'm not exactly alone anymore."

And there it was. Rose had been a little distracted lately but also in a good mood, and a noticeable good mood was a rare occurrence for Rose Black. Avery had thought there might be a boy involved and that opened up a whole different can of worms that Avery wasn't prepared to deal with. She'd missed the period talk with Rose, missed details of her first crush, first dance, and first kiss. Now that she was faced with the potential love life of her eighteen-year-old daughter, she understood just how much she had missed.

"What do you mean?" Avery asked.

Rose bit at her lip, as if she regretted having said anything.

"I…well, I might have met someone."

She said it casually and a bit dismissively, making it clear that she had no interest in talking about it.

"Oh yeah?" Avery asked. "When was this?"

"About a month ago," Rose said.

Exactly the amount of time I've been noticing her better moods, Avery thought. Sometimes it was eerie how her detective skills overlaid her personal life.

4

"But…he's not living here, is he?" Rose asked.

"No, Mom. But he might be here a lot."

"That's not the sort of thing the mother of an eighteen-year-old wants to hear," Avery said.

"God, Mom. It'll be okay."

Avery knew she should leave it alone. If Rose wanted to talk to her about this guy, she'd do it on her own time. Pressuring her would only make it worse.

But again, her work instinct took over and she couldn't help herself from asking more questions.

"Can I meet him?"

"Um, absolutely not. Not yet, anyway."

Avery sensed the opportunity to go deeper into the conversation—the awkward conversation about protected sex and the risk of diseases and teenage pregnancy. But she almost felt like she didn't have that right, given their strained relationship.

Being a Homicide detective, though, it was impossible *not* to worry. She knew the caliber of men out there. She had seen not just murders but severe domestic abuse cases. And while this guy in Rose's life might be a perfect gentleman, it was much easier for Rose to assume that he was a threat.

At some point, though, didn't she have to trust her daughter's instincts? Hadn't she just complimented Rose on how well she had turned out despite her upbringing?

"Just be careful," Avery said.

Rose was clearly embarrassed. She rolled her eyes and started unpacking DVDs in the small living room that joined the kitchen.

"What about you?" Rose asked. "Don't you ever get tired of being alone? You know…Dad's still alone, too."

"I'm aware of that," Avery said. "But that's none of my business."

"He's your ex-husband," Rose pointed out. "And he's my father. So yeah, he sort of *is* your business. It might do you some good to see him."

"That wouldn't be good for either of us," Avery replied. "If you'd ask him, I'm sure he'd tell you the same thing."

Avery knew this was true. While they had never talked about getting back together, there was an unspoken agreement between them—something they'd felt in the air ever since she'd lost her job as an attorney and had basically ruined her life in the weeks that followed. They would tolerate one another for Rose. Although there were mutual feelings of love and respect there, they both knew there would be no getting back together. Jack was only worried about the same thing she was worried about. He wanted Avery spending more time with Rose. And it was up to her to figure out how to do that. She'd spent time coming up with a plan over the last few weeks and although it would require sacrifice on her part, she was ready to try.

Sensing that the touchy topic of Jack was already passing over like a storm cloud, Avery tried broaching the topic of that sacrifice. There was no way to subtly get to it, so she just came out and said it.

"I was thinking about maybe asking for a lighter workload for the next few months. I figured you and I should really give things a real chance."

Rose paused for a minute. She looked taken aback, genuinely surprised. She gave a little nod of acknowledgment and went back to unpacking. She made a little *hmmph* sound.

"What?" Avery asked.

"But you love your work."

"I do," Avery agreed. "But I've been thinking of transferring out of Homicide. If I did that, my schedule would be freed up a bit."

Rose now stopped unpacking completely. A range of expressions crossed her face in the space of a second. Avery was pleased to see that one looked very much like hope.

"Mom, you don't have to do that." Her voice was soft and unguarded, almost like the little girl Avery could easily remember. "That's like uprooting your life."

"No it's not. I'm getting older and realizing that I missed out on a lot of family stuff. It's what I need to do to move on…to get better."

Rose sat down on the couch, littered with boxes and stray clothes. She looked up to Avery, that gleam of hope still on her face.

"Are you sure that's what you want?" she asked.

"I don't know. Maybe."

"Also," Rose said, "I see where I get my awesome ability to swerve subjects. You hopped off of being alone all the time pretty quickly."

"You noticed that, did you?"

"I did. And to be honest, I think Dad has, too."

"Rose—"

Rose turned to her.

"He misses you, Mom."

Avery slouched. She stood there, quiet for a moment, unable to respond.

6

"I miss him sometimes, too," Avery admitted. "Just not enough to call him up and dredge up the past."

He misses you, Mom.

Avery let that sink in. She rarely thought of Jack in any real sort of romantic sense. She had told the truth, though: She *did* miss him. She missed Jack's weird sense of humor, the way his body always seemed just a little too cold in the mornings, how his need for sex was almost comically predictable. More than anything, though, she missed watching him be an excellent father. But that was all gone now, part of a life that Avery was trying very hard to put behind her.

Still, she couldn't help but wonder what might have been, realizing that she'd had the chance for a great life. A life with picket fences, school fundraisers, lazy Sunday afternoons in the backyard.

But the chance for that was gone. Rose had missed out on that perfect picture and Avery still blamed herself.

"Mom?"

"Sorry, Rose. I just don't see your dad and I mending things, you know? Besides," she added, and took a deep breath, bracing herself for Rose's reaction, "maybe you aren't the only one that's met someone."

Rose turned to her, and Avery was relieved to see her smile. She looked to her mother with the sort of devilish grin girlfriends might share over cocktails while talking about men. It warmed Avery's heart in a way she was not prepared for, nor could she explain.

"What?" Rose asked, feigning shock. "You? Details, please."

"There are no details yet."

"Well, who is it?"

Avery chuckled, realizing how silly it would seem. She almost didn't say it. Hell, she had barely even told the guy how she felt. To voice it in front of her daughter would be a bit surreal.

Still, she and Rose were making progress. No sense in stifling it because of her own embarrassment of having feelings for a man that was not Rose's father.

"It's a man I work with. Ramirez."

"Have you guys hooked up?"

"Rose!"

Rose shrugged. "Hey…you wanted an open and honest relationship with your daughter, right?"

"Yes, I suppose I do," she said with a smile. "And no…we have not *hooked up.* But I'm sort of falling for him. He's nice.

Funny, sexy, and has this sort of charm to him that used to annoy me but now…it's sort of appealing."

"Does he feel the same?" Rose asked.

"He does. Or…he did. I think I blew it. He's been patient but I think his patience ran out." What she kept to herself was that she had made the decision to tell Ramirez how she felt but had not yet summoned up the nerve to do so.

"Did you push him away?" Rose asked.

Avery smiled.

"Damn, you're observant."

"I'm telling you…it's genetics."

Rose grinned again, seeming to have forgotten about unpacking for the moment.

"Go for it, Mom!"

"Oh my God."

Rose laughed and Avery soon joined in. It was easily the most vulnerable they had been with one another since they had started working toward repairing their relationship. Suddenly, the idea of taking a step back from Homicide and taking some time off from work seemed like a necessity rather than just a hopeful idea.

"Are you doing anything this weekend?" Avery asked.

"Unpacking. Maybe a date with Ma—the guy who shall remain nameless for now."

"How about a girls' day with your mom tomorrow? Lunch, a movie, pedicures."

Rose wrinkled her nose at the idea but then seemed to seriously consider it. "Do I get to choose the movie?"

"If you must."

"Sounds like fun," Rose said with an edge of excitement. "Count me in."

"Great," Avery said. She then felt a prompting—a need to ask something that felt weird but something that would be pivotal to their relationship going forward. Knowing what she about to ask her daughter was humbling but also, in a very strange way, freeing.

"So you'd be okay with me moving on?" Avery asked.

"What do you mean?" Rose asked. "From Dad?"

"Yes. From your dad and that whole part of my life—the part of my life that made things rough for all of us. A big part of me moving on from that is not being chained by the guilt of what might have been. And I have to move away from your dad for that. I'll always love him and respect him for raising you while I wasn't there but he's a big part of the life that I need to get away from. Do you get that?"

"I do," Rose said. Her voice had gone soft and vulnerable again. Hearing it made Avery want to go over to the couch and hug her. "And you don't need my permission, Mom," Rose continued. "I know you're trying. I can see it. I really can."

For the third time in fifteen minutes, Avery felt herself inching toward tears. She sighed, and pushed the urge to cry away.

"How'd you turn out to be so good?" Avery asked.

"Genetics," Rose said. "You might have made some mistakes, Mom. But you've always been kind of a badass."

Before Avery had time to even form a response, Rose stepped forward and hugged her. It was a genuine embrace—something she had not felt from her daughter in quite a while.

This time, Avery let the tears come.

She could not remember the last time she had been quite this happy. For the first time in a very long time, she felt as if she were truly taking steps to escaping the mistakes of her past.

A big part of that would be talking to Ramirez and letting him know that she was done with hiding what had been growing between them. She wanted to be with him—whatever that looked like. Suddenly, with her daughter's arms around her, Avery could not wait to have that discussion with him.

In fact, she hoped it went far beyond a discussion. She hoped they'd end up doing much more than simply talking, finally letting the tension that had been building between them have its way.

9

CHAPTER TWO

She met with Ramirez three hours later, just after his shift had ended. He'd answered her call eagerly enough but had sounded tired. That's why they had elected to meet alongside the Charles River, on one of the many benches that overlooked it from the walking paths around the eastern lip of the river.

As she strolled up to the bench they had agreed upon, she saw that he had just gotten there. He was sitting down, looking out across the river. The tiredness in his voice showed on his face. He looked peaceful, though. She'd noticed this about him on numerous occasions, how he would get silent and introspective whenever presented with a scenic view of the city.

She approached him and he turned to her when he heard her footfalls. He flashed his winning smile and just like that, he no longer looked tired. One of the many things Avery liked about Ramirez was the way he made her feel whenever he looked at her. It was clear that there was more than simple attraction there; he looked at her with appreciation and respect. That, plus the fact that he told her that she was beautiful on a routine basis, made her feel safer and more desired than she could ever remember feeling.

"Long day?" Avery asked him as she joined him on the bench.

"Not really," Ramirez said. "It was filled with busy work. Noise complaints. A fight at a bar that got a little bloody. And I shit you not, I even got a call about a dog that had chased a kid up a tree."

"A kid?"

"A kid," Ramirez said. "The glamorous life of a detective when the city is quiet and boring."

They both looked out over the river in a silence that, over the last few weeks, had started to grow comfortable. While they were not technically an item, they had come to appreciate the time together that wasn't filled with talk just for the sake of talk. Slowly and deliberately, Avery reached over and took his hand.

"Walk with me, would you?"

"Sure," he said, giving her hand a squeeze.

Even hand holding was something monumental to Avery. She and Ramirez held hands frequently and had kissed briefly on a few occasions—but intentionally holding his hand was out of her comfort zone.

But it's getting comfortable, she thought as they started walking. *Hell, it's* been *comfortable for some time now.*

"Are you okay?" Ramirez asked.

"I am," she said. "I had a really good day with Rose."

"Things finally starting to feel normal there?" he asked.

"Far from normal," Avery said. "But it's getting there. And speaking of getting there…"

She paused, confused why it was so hard for her to say what she wanted to say. Due to her past, she knew she was emotionally strong…so why was it so hard to actually express herself when it was important?

"This is going to sound cheesy," Avery said. "So please bear with me and keep my extreme vulnerability in mind."

"Okay…" Ramirez said, clearly confused.

"I've known for quite some time that I need to make some changes. A big part of that came in trying to fix things with Rose. But there are other things, too. Things I've been almost frightened to admit to myself."

"Like what?" Ramirez said.

She could tell that he was getting a little uncomfortable. They'd been transparent with one another before, but never quite to this extent. This was much harder than she had expected.

"Look…I know I've basically ruined things between us," Avery said. "You showed extreme patience and understanding as I worked through my crap. And I know I kept luring you in a little at a time only to push you away."

"That would be accurate, yes," Ramirez said with a bit of humor.

"I can't apologize enough for that," Avery said. "And if you could find it in your heart to look past my hesitancy and my fears…I'd really like to have another chance."

"A chance for what?" Ramirez said.

He's going to make me come out and say it, she said. *And I kind of deserve this treatment.*

The evening was unraveling into dusk and there were only a scant few people out along the sidewalks and trails that wound around the river. It was a picturesque scene, like something out of one of those movies she usually hated to watch.

"A chance for *us,*" Avery said.

Ramirez stopped walking but kept her hand in his. He looked to her with his dark brown eyes and held her gaze. "It can't be a chance," he said. "It has to be a real thing. A surefire thing. I can't keep having you push and push, always keeping me guessing."

"I know."

"So if you can let me know what you mean by *us*, then I'll consider it."

She couldn't tell if he was being serious or just trying to give her a hard time. She broke their eye contact and gave his hands a squeeze.

"Damn," she said. "You're going to make this hard on me, aren't you?"

"Well, I think I—"

She interrupted him by pulling him to her and kissing him. In the past, their kisses had been brief, awkward, and filled with her usual hesitancy. But now she lost herself to it. She drew him as close as their bodies would allow and kissed him with the most passion she'd put into any sort of physical contact since the last happy year of marriage with Jack.

Ramirez didn't bother trying to fight it. She knew he had been wanting this for a while now and she could feel the eagerness running through him.

They kissed like love-struck teenagers by the side of the Charles River. It was a soft yet heated kiss that thrummed with the sexual frustration that had been blooming between them for several months.

When their tongues met, Avery felt a surge of energy pass through her—energy that she knew she wanted to use up in a very certain way.

She broke the kiss and leaned her forehead into his. They looked to one another for several seconds in that posture, enjoying the silence and the weight of what they had just done. A line had been crossed. And in the tense silence, they both sensed that there were still many more to cross.

"You're sure about this?" Ramirez asked.

"I am. And I'm sorry it took me so long to realize it."

He drew her close and hugged her. She felt something like relief in his body, like a huge weight had been lifted from him.

"I'd like to give it a try," Ramirez said.

He broke the hug and kissed her again, softly, on the side of the mouth.

"I think we need to celebrate the occasion. You want to get dinner?"

She sighed and gave a shaky smile. She had already broken through an emotional barrier by confessing her feelings to him. What harm could it do to continue being blatantly honest with him now?

"I do think we need to celebrate," she said. "But right now, at this very moment, I'm not too interested in dinner."

"So what do you want to do?" he asked.

His obliviousness was beyond charming. She leaned in and whispered into his ear, enjoying the feel of him against her and the smell of his skin.

"Let's go to your place."

He pulled away and looked at her with the same seriousness as before, but now there was something else there, too. It was something she had seen in his eyes from time to time—something that looked very much like excitement and was born out of a physical need.

"Yeah?" he said uncertainly.

"Yeah," she said.

As they hurried across the grass, toward the parking lot where they had both parked their cars, they were giggling like children. It was fitting, as Avery could not recall the last time she had felt so liberated, excited, and free.

***

The passion they had experienced while along the river was still there as Ramirez unlocked his apartment door. There was a part of Avery that wanted to jump him right there and then, before he even had time to shut the door behind him. They'd lightly pawed at one another the whole ride to his place and now that they were there, Avery felt like they were on the precipice of something monumental.

When Ramirez closed the door and locked it, Avery was surprised when he didn't come to her right away. Instead, he walked through the living room and into his modest kitchen, where he poured himself a glass of water.

"Water?" he asked.

"No thanks," she said.

He drank from his glass and looked out the kitchen window. Night had fallen and the city lights sparkled through the glass.

Avery joined him in the kitchen and playfully took the glass of water from him. "What's the matter?" she asked.

"I don't want to say," he said.

"Do you...well, have you changed your mind about me?" she asked. "Did all the waiting make you stop wanting me?"

"God no," he said. He put his arms around her waist and she could see him trying to form the right words.

"We can wait," she said, hoping he wouldn't take her up on it.

"No," he said, a little urgently. "It's just….shit, I don't know."

This was a surprise to Avery. With all of his masterful flirtation and seductive talk over the last few months, she was sure he would have been a little aggressive when and if the time ever came. But right now, he seemed unsure of himself—almost nervous.

She leaned in and kissed the corner of his jaw. He sighed and leaned in against her.

"What is it?" she asked, her lips brushing his skin as she spoke.

"It's just that this is real now, you know? This isn't just some one-night stand. This is for real. I care about you a lot, Avery. I really do. And I don't want to rush things."

"We've been dancing around this for the last four months," she said. "I don't think that's rushing."

"Good point," he said. He kissed her on the cheek, then on the little bit of shoulder her T-shirt was showing. His lips then found her neck and when he kissed her there, she thought she might collapse to the floor right on the spot, pulling him down with her.

"Ramirez?" she said, still playfully refusing to use his first name.

"Yeah?" he asked, his face still brushing against her neck and applying kisses.

"Take me to the bedroom."

He pulled her close, hoisted her up, and allowed her to wrap her legs around his waist. They started kissing then and he obeyed her. He slowly carried her to the bedroom and by the time he shut the bedroom door, Avery was so lost in the moment that she never even heard it close.

All she was aware of was his hands, his mouth, his well-toned body pressing against hers as he laid her down on the bed.

He broke their kiss long enough to ask: "Are you sure about this?"

And if she needed one more reason to want him, that was it. He genuinely cared about her and did not want to ruin what they had.

She nodded and pulled him down onto her.

And then for a while, she was not a frustrated Homicide detective or a struggling mother, or a daughter who had watched her mother die at her father's hands. She was just Avery Black then…a woman like any other woman, enjoying the pleasures life had to offer.

She'd almost forgotten what that was like.

And once she started to get acquainted with them, she vowed to herself that she would never allow herself to forget them again.

14

CHAPTER THREE

Avery opened her eyes and looked at the unfamiliar ceiling over her head. The muted light of dawn came in through the bedroom window, spilling across her mostly naked body. It also painted Ramirez's naked back beside her. She turned over slightly and smiled sleepily. He was still asleep, his face turned away from her.

They'd made love twice the night before, taking two hours between each session to make a quick dinner and discuss how sleeping together could complicate their working relationship if they weren't careful. It had been close to midnight when they had finally drifted off side by side. Avery had been drowsy and could not remember when she'd fallen asleep but she *did* remember his arm around her waist.

She wanted that again…that feeling of being wanted and being secure. She thought about running her fingertips along the base of his spine (as well as a few other places, perhaps) just to wake him up so he could hold her.

But she did not get the chance. The text alarm of her phone went off. So did Ramirez's. They pinged together, an occasion that could only mean one thing: it was work-related.

Ramirez sat up quickly. When he did, the sheet slid off of him and revealed everything. Avery snuck a peek, unable to resist herself. He grabbed his phone from the bedside table and looked at it with bleary eyes. While he did this, Avery retrieved her own phone from the pile of clothes on the floor.

The text was from Dylan Connelly, the A1 Homicide Supervisor. In Connelly's typical fashion, the message was direct and to the point:

Body discovered. Burned badly. Maybe trauma to head.
Get your ass to abandoned construction lot on Kirkley St NOW.

"Well, that's nice to wake up to first thing in the morning," she grumbled.

Ramirez climbed off the bed, still completely naked, and hunkered down on the floor with her. He pulled her close to him and said, "Yeah, *this* is nice to wake up to first thing in the morning."

She leaned into him, a little alarmed at how insanely content she was in that moment. She grumbled again and got to her feet.

15

"Shit," she said. "We're going to be late to the scene. I need to get my car *and* get back home for a change of clothes."

"We'll be okay," Ramirez said as he started getting dressed. "I'll text back in few minutes, while we're on the way to your car. You space yours out. Maybe the text sound didn't wake you. Maybe it took me calling you to wake you up."

"That sounds deceptive," she said, sliding her shirt on.

"That's *clever* is what it is," he said.

They smiled at each other as they finished getting dressed. They then went into the bathroom, where Avery did her best to make sense of her hair while Ramirez brushed his teeth. They hurried to the kitchen and Avery threw together two bowls of cereal.

"As you can see," she said, "I'm quite the cook."

He hugged her from behind and seemed to breathe her in. "Are we going to be okay?" he asked. "We can make this work, right?"

"I think so," she said. "Let's go out there and give it a try."

They wolfed down their cereal, spending most of the time looking at one another, trying to gauge the other's reaction to what had happened last night. From what Avery could tell, he was just as happy as she was.

They headed out the front door but before Ramirez closed it behind them, he stopped. "Wait, back inside for a minute."

Confused, she stepped back inside.

"Inside," he said, "we're off the clock. Not really officially partners, right?"

"Right," Avery said.

"So I can do this one more time," he said.

He leaned in and kissed her. It was a dizzying kiss, one with enough force to cause her knees to sag a bit. She playfully pushed him away. "Like I said before," she said, "don't start. Not unless you intend to finish."

"Rain check," he said. He then led her outside and closed the door behind them this time. "Okay, on the clock now. Lead the way, Detective Black."

***

They went with Ramirez's plan. She did not return Connelly's text for another sixteen minutes. By that time, she was nearly back to her apartment and still quite giddy over the way last night had played out. She managed to get dressed, grab coffee, and hit the street again in less than ten minutes. The result, of course, was

16

arriving at the scene on Kirkley Street roughly half an hour later than Connelly would have preferred.

There were several officers already milling around. They were all familiar faces, faces that she had come to know and respect since becoming a Homicide detective. The looks on their faces this morning clued her in to the fact that this was going to be a very long and bitter morning.

One of the people she saw in attendance was Mike O'Malley. She found it alarming that the captain would be out here so soon. As the head over most of Boston PD, he was rarely seen in the hustle and bustle of everyday crime scenes, no matter how vile they might be. O'Malley was currently speaking to two other officers, one of which was Finley. Avery had grown to respect Finley as an officer even though he tended to be a little too aloof for her liking.

She spotted Ramirez right away; he was chatting with Connelly on the far side of the abandoned lot.

As she made her way over to Ramirez and Connelly, she took in the scene as best she could. She'd been through this part of town several times but had never paid it any real attention. It was one of the many financial blights on this end of town, an area where enthusiastic developers had sunk tons of money into property only to see the property lose its value and potential buyers quickly run away. Once the housing efforts had shut down, the area had gone back to ruin. And it seemed to fit well with the surroundings.

Twin smokestacks could be seen in the distance, rising up like blemished giants. They both sent broken plumes of smoke into the air, giving the morning an overcast sort of feel—but only in this part of town. On the other side of the abandoned lot, Avery could see the edges of what could have been a promising little creek that would have run along behind the properties of upper-middle-class houses. Now, it was taken over by an overgrowth of weeds and brambles. Plastic bags, snack wrappers, and other litter were stuck in the dead weeds. The shallow banks were muddy and neglected, adding a whole new stagnant level to the sludge of it all.

Overall, this area had become a part of town that just about anyone would gladly skip over. Avery knew the feeling; taking it all in as she closed in on Ramirez and Connelly, the area instantly made her feel burdened.

An area like this can't be a coincidence, she thought. *If someone killed here or even just dumped a body here, it has to have some significance…either to the murder itself or to the killer.*

Immediately to the left of Finley and Ramirez, an officer had just finished putting up thin red stakes to border off a rectangular section of the lot. As Avery's eyes fell on what rested inside that rectangle, Connelly's voice boomed at her from just a few feet away.

"Damn, Black…what took you so long?"

"Sorry," she said. "I slept right through the text buzz. Ramirez called me and woke me up."

"Well, you aren't late because you were busy doing your hair or makeup, that's for damned sure," Connelly remarked.

"She doesn't need makeup," Ramirez said. "That shit's for girls."

"Thanks, guys," Avery said.

"Whatever," Connelly said. "So what do you think of *this*?" he asked, nodding down to the rectangle drawn out by the red stakes.

Inside of the marked-off area, she saw what she assumed were human remains. Most of what she saw was a skeletal structure but it seemed to gleam. There was no age to it. It was unmistakably a skeleton that had very recently been robbed of its flesh. All around it was what appeared to be ash or some sort of grime. Here and there, she saw what may have been muscle and tissue clinging to the skeleton, particularly around the legs and the ribs.

"What the hell happened?" she asked.

"Well, what a great question for our best detective to start with," Connelly said. "But here's what we know so far. About an hour and fifteen minutes ago, a woman out for her morning run put in a call about what she described as something that looked like a weird Satanic ritual. It led us to this."

Avery hunkered down by the red markers and peered into the area. An hour and ten minutes ago. That meant that if the black stuff around the skeleton *was* ash, this skeleton had been covered in skin at least an hour and a half ago. But that didn't seem likely. It would take some sick determination and planning to kill someone and then miraculously burn them down to nothing but bone in such a short amount of time. In fact, she thought it would be next to impossible.

"Anyone have evidence gloves?" she asked.

"One second," Ramirez said.

As he ran to Finley and the other officers who had stepped back to allow Avery some room, she also noticed a smell in the area. It was faint but noticeable—a chemical smell that was almost like bleach to her nose.

"Anyone else smell that?" she asked.

"Some sort of chemical, right?" Connelly asked. "We figure a chemical-induced burn is the only way you can fry a body like this one so quickly."

"I'm not thinking the burn was done here," she said.

"How can you be so sure?" Connelly asked.

I'm not, she thought. *But the only thing that makes sense to me at first guess seems pretty damned absurd.*

"Avery—" Connelly said.

"One second," she said. "I'm thinking."

"Jesus…"

She ignored him, looking at the ash and the skeleton with an investigative eye. *No…the body couldn't have been burned here. There are no scorch marks around the body. A burning person would flail and run about wildly. Nothing here is burned at all. The only sign of a fire of any kind are these ashes. So why would a killer burn the body and then bring it back here? Maybe this is where he took the victim…*

The possibilities were endless. One of the possibilities, Avery thought, was that perhaps the skeleton was the property of a medical lab somewhere and this was just some stupid sick prank. But given the location and the brazenness of the act, she doubted this was the case.

Ramirez returned with a pair of latex evidence gloves. Avery slipped them on and reached down to the ash. She gripped just a small bit of it between her pointer finger and thumb. She rubbed her fingers together and brought it to her face. She sniffed at it and looked at it closely. It looked like standard ash but possessed traces of the chemical smell.

"We need to have this ash analyzed," Avery said. "If there was a chemical involved, there's a good chance that there are still trace amounts in the ashes."

"There's a forensics team on the way as we speak," Connelly said.

Slowly, Avery got to her feet and removed the latex gloves. O'Malley and Finley came over and Avery wasn't surprised to see Finley keep his distance from the skeleton and ashes. He looked at them as if the skeleton might jump out at him at any moment.

"I'm working with the city to get footage from every security camera within a six-block radius," O'Malley said. "Because there aren't many of them in this part of town, it shouldn't take too long."

"It might not be a bad idea to also get the numbers of any companies that sell highly flammable chemicals," Avery pointed out.

"That could be millions of places," Connelly said.

"No, she's right," O'Malley said. "This burn wasn't done with just a household cleaner or spray. This was a concentrated chemical, I'd say. Finley, can you start working on that?"

"Yes, sir," Finley said, clearly glad to have a reason to leave the scene.

"Black and Ramirez...this is your case now," O'Malley said. "Work with Connelly to get a team on this ASAP."

"Got it," Ramirez said.

"And Black, let's make sure we're prompt for the rest of this thing. You showing up late this morning set us back fifteen minutes."

Avery nodded, not allowing herself to get baited into an argument. She knew that most of the men above her were still looking for any small thing to bust her on. And she was fine with that. Given her sordid history, she almost expected it.

As she started to step away from the red markers, she noticed something else several yards to the right. She'd seen it when she first approached the skeletal remains but had disregarded it as simple litter. But now as she walked closer to the detritus, she saw what looked to be the broken shards of something. It looked almost like glass, possibly something that had been fired in a kiln at some point. She walked over to it, getting a better view of the murky and stagnant creek along the back of the lot.

"Did anyone take note of this?" she asked.

Connelly looked over, barely interested.

"Just litter," he said.

Avery shook her head.

"I don't think so," she said.

She slipped the latex gloves back on and picked up a piece of it. Upon closer inspection, she saw that whatever the object had been, it had been made of glass, not a ceramic material. There didn't seem to be any dust or weathered wear and tear on the fragments. There were seven larger chunks, about the size of her palm, and then countless little slivers of it all over the ground. Aside from having been shattered, whatever had been broken looked to be fairly new.

"Whatever this is, it hasn't been here for very long," she said. "Make sure forensics checks this for prints."

"I'll sic forensics on it," Connelly said in a tone that indicated he did not appreciate taking orders. "Now, you two...make sure you get to the A1 within the next half an hour. I'll make some calls and have a team waiting for you in the conference room. This scene is less than two hours old; I'd like to nail this asshole before he gets too much of a head start."

Avery took one final look at the skeleton. Without the cover of flesh, it looked like it was smiling. To Avery, it was almost as if the killer were smiling at her, biting back a taunting laugh. And it wasn't just the sight of a newly stripped skeleton that made her feel a sense of foreboding and doom. It was the location, the almost perfectly sculpted mounds of ash around the bones, the purposefully unhidden remains, and the chemical smell.

It all seemed to point to something precise. It pointed to vast intention and planning. And as far as Avery was concerned, that could only mean one thing: whoever did this would certainly do it again.

CHAPTER FOUR

Forty minutes later, Avery stepped into the central conference room in the A1 headquarters. It was already filled with an assortment of officers and experts, totaling twelve in all, and she knew most of them, though not as well as Ramirez or Finley. She supposed that was her own fault. After Ramirez had been assigned to her as a partner, she had not gone out of her way to make friends. It seemed like a silly thing to do as a Homicide detective.

As they all took their seats around the table (except for Avery, who always preferred to stand), one of the officers she did not know started passing out printed copies of the scant information they had so far—pictures of the crime scene and a sheet of bullet points of what they knew about the scene. Avery scanned one and found it succinct.

She noted that as everyone started to take their seats, Ramirez sat in front of her. She looked down at him and realized that she had instinctively stepped closer to him. She also found that she wanted to rest her hand on his shoulder, just to touch him. She backed away, noticing that Finley was looking oddly at her.

Shit, she thought. *Is it that obvious?*

She went back to busying herself with rereading the notes. As she did so, O'Malley and Connelly entered the room. O'Malley closed the door and went to the front of the room. Before he started speaking, the murmurs and conversation within the room died down. Avery watched him with great appreciation and respect. He was the sort of man who could take charge of a room by simply clearing his throat or letting it be known that he was about to speak.

"Thanks for scrambling together so quickly," O'Malley said. "You have in your hands everything we know about this case so far with one exception. I had city workers pull everything they could from traffic light cameras in the area. Two of the four cameras show a woman walking her dog. And that's all we got."

"There's one other thing," one of the officers at the table said. Avery knew this man's name was Mosely, but that was about all she knew about him. "I got word two minutes before stepping into this meeting that dispatch fielded a call this morning from an elderly man claiming that he saw what he described as 'a creepy tall man' walking in that area. He said he was tucking some sort of a bag under a long coat. Dispatch took note of it but assumed it was just a nosy old man with nothing better to do. But then when this burn case kicked off this morning, they pinged me on it."

"Do we have this old man's contact information?" Avery asked.

Connelly shot her an annoyed look. She supposed he thought she was speaking out of turn—even though he had told her no more than forty-five minutes ago that this was her case.

"We do," Mosely answered.

"I want someone on the phone with him the moment this meeting is over," O'Malley said. "Finley…where are we on a list of places that sell chemicals that can burn this fiercely in such a short time?"

"I've got three places within twenty miles. Two of them are e-mailing me a list of chemicals that could do such a thing and whether or not they keep it in stock."

Avery listened to the back-and-forth, taking mental notes and trying to sort them into the appropriate slots. With each new bit of information, the more sense the odd crime scene from this morning started to make. Although, really, there wasn't too much sense to be made at this point.

"We still have no idea who the victim is," O'Malley said. "We're going to have to go on dental records alone on this one unless we can make some sort of connection with the footage from the traffic cameras." He then looked to Avery and gestured her to the front of the table. "Detective Black is the head on this one so everything you find from here on out will go directly to her."

Avery joined him up front and scanned the table. Her eyes landed on Jane Parks, one of the lead investigators on forensics. "Do we have any results from the broken glass shards?" she asked.

"Not yet," Parks said. "We know for certain that there were no fingerprints, though. But we're still working to find out what the object was. So far we can only imagine it might have been some sort of knickknack that is in no way related to the crime."

"And what is the opinion of forensics in regards to the fire?" Avery asked. "Are you also in agreement that this was no casual burning?"

"Yes. The ash is still being studied, but it's obvious that no standard fire could burn human flesh so thoroughly. There were barely even any charred remains on the bones and the bones themselves almost look pristine, showing no signs of scorching."

"And can you describe to us what the usual process of a body burning might be?" Avery asked.

"Well, there's nothing typical about burning a body unless you're cremating it," Parks said. "But let's say a body is trapped in a burning house and is lit on fire that way. Body fat acts like a sort of fuel once the skin is burned away, which keeps the fire going. Almost like a candle, you know? But this burn was quick and very succinct…probably so intense that it vaporized the fat before it could even act as a fuel."

"How long would it take a body to burn down to nothing more than bone?" Avery asked.

"Well, there are several determining factors," Parks said. "But anywhere between five to seven hours is an accurate number. Slow and controlled burns, like the ones used at crematoriums, can take up to eight hours."

"And this one burned in less than an hour and a half?" Connelly asked.

"Yes, that's the assumption," Parks said.

The conference room was awash in murmurs of disgust and awe. Avery understood it. It was hard to wrap her mind around it.

"Or," Avery said, "the body was burned elsewhere and the remains were dumped in that lot this morning."

"But that skeleton…that was a new skeleton," Parks said. "It wasn't without its skin, muscle, tissues, and so on for very long. Not long at all."

"Can you make an educated guess as to how long ago the body was burned?" Avery asked.

"Surely no more than a day or so."

"So this took planning and some head knowledge on the killer's part," Avery said. "He'd have to know a lot about burning bodies. And being that he made no attempt to hide the remains as well as killed the victim in such a startling way…that denotes a few things. And the thing that I fear the most is that this is likely the first of many."

"What do you mean?" Connelly asked.

She felt all eyes in the room turn to her.

"I mean that this is probably the work of a serial killer."

A heavy silence blanketed the room.

"What are you talking about?" Connelly asked. "There's no evidence to support that."

"Nothing obvious," Avery admitted. "But he wanted the remains to be found. He made no attempt to hide them in that lot. There was a creek right along the back of the property. He could have dumped it all there. More than that, there was ash. Why dump ash at the scene when you could easily dispose of it at home? The planning and the method of the killing…he took great pride and pleasure in this. He wanted the remains found and speculated over. And that holds the marks of a serial killer."

24

She felt the room stare back at her, felt a solemn air descend, and she knew they were thinking the same thing she was: this was evolving from an odd case involving an impromptu cremation to a time-sensitive hunt for a serial killer.

CHAPTER FIVE

After the tension of the meeting, Avery was glad to find herself back behind the wheel of her car with Ramirez in the passenger seat. There was an odd bit of silence between them that made her uneasy. Had she really been so naïve to think that sleeping together was not going to alter their working relationship?

Was it a mistake?

It was starting to feel like it. The fact that the sex had been pretty close to mind-blowing made it hard to accept, though.

"While we have a second," Ramirez said, "are we going to talk about last night?"

"We can," Avery said. "What do you want to talk about?"

"Well, at the risk of sounding like a stereotypical male, I was wondering if it was a one-time thing or if we were going to do it again."

"I don't know," Avery said.

"Regretting it already?" he asked.

"No," she said. "No regrets. It's just that in the moment, I wasn't thinking about how it would affect our working relationship."

"I figure it can't hurt it," Ramirez said. "All jokes aside, you and I have been dancing around this physical chemistry for months now. We finally did something about it, so the tension should be gone, right?"

"You'd think so," Avery said with a sly smile.

"It's not for you?"

She thought for a while and then shrugged. "I don't know. And quite frankly, I'm not sure I'm ready to talk about it yet."

"Fair enough. We *are* sort of in the middle of what looks to be a majorly fucked up case."

"Yes, we are," she said. "Did you get the e-mail from the precinct? What else do we know about our witness other than his address?"

Ramirez looked to his phone and pulled up his e-mail. "Got it," he said. "Our witness is Donald Greer, eighty-one years of age. Retired. He lives in an apartment roughly half a mile away from the crime scene. He's a widower who worked for fifty-five years as a shipyard supervisor after getting two toes blown off in Vietnam."

"And how did he happen to see the killer?" Avery asked.

"That we don't know yet. But I guess it's our job to find out, right?"

"Right," she said.

Silence fell on them again. She felt the instinct to reach out and take his hand but thought better of it. It was best to keep things strictly professional. Maybe they *would* end up in bed together again and maybe things would even progress to more than that—to something more emotional and concrete.

But none of that mattered now. Now, they had a job to do and anything evolving within their personal lives would just have to be put on hold.

***

Donald Greer showed all eighty-one years of his age. His hair was a frazzled shock of white atop his head and his teeth were slightly discolored from age and improper care. Still, he was clearly glad to have company as he invited Avery and Ramirez into his home. When he smiled at them, it was so genuine and wide that the unsightly condition of his teeth seemed to disappear.

"Can I get you some coffee or tea?" he asked them as they came in.

"No, thank you," Avery said.

Somewhere else in the house, a dog barked. It was a smaller dog, and one with a bark that suggested it might be just about as old as Donald.

"So is this about that man I saw this morning?" Donald asked. He plopped himself down into an armchair in the living room.

"Yes, sir, it is," Avery said. "We were told that you saw a tall man that appeared to be hiding something under his—"

The dog that was located somewhere in the back of the apartment started to bark even more. Its yaps were loud and sort of grizzled.

"*Shut it, Daisy!*" Donald said. The dog went silent, giving a little whimper. Donald shook his head and gave a chuckle. "Daisy loves company," he said. "But she's getting old and tends to pee on people when she gets too excited, so I had to lock her up for your visit. I was out walking her this morning when I saw that man."

"How far do you walk her?" Avery asked.

"Oh, Daisy and I walk at least a mile and a half just about every morning. My ticker isn't as strong as it used to be. The doctor says I need to walk as much as possible. It's supposed to keep my joints in top order, too."

"I see," Avery said. "Do you take the same route every morning?"

27

"No. We switch it up from time to time. We have about five different routes we take."

"And where were you when you saw the man this morning?"

"Out on Kirkley. Me and Daisy had just come around the corner of Spring Street. That part of town is *always* empty in the mornings. A few work trucks here and there but that's about it. I think we've passed two or three people on Kirkley in the last month or so…and they were all walking their dogs. You don't even get any of those masochistic people that like to run out in this area."

It was obvious by the way he chatted that Donald Greer did not get many visitors. He was overly chatty and spoke very loudly. Avery wondered if it was because age had affected his hearing or if his ears were shot from listening to Daisy raise hell all day.

"And was this man coming or going?" Avery asked.

"Coming, I think. I'm not sure. He was a good ways ahead of me and he seemed to sort of stop for a second when I got on Kirkley. I think he knew I was there, behind him. He started walking again, sort of fast, and then just sort of disappeared into the fog. Maybe he took one of those side streets along Kirkley."

"Was he maybe walking a dog?" Ramirez asked.

"Nope. I would have known. Daisy goes ballistic when she sees another dog or even smells one in the area. But she stayed just as quiet as always."

"Do you have any idea what he might have been holding under that jacket you say he was wearing?"

"I couldn't see," Donald said. "I just saw him shifting something under it. But the fog this morning was just too thick."

"And what about the coat he was wearing?" Avery asked. "What kind was it?"

Before he could answer, they were interrupted by Ramirez's cell phone. He answered it and stepped away, speaking quietly into it.

"The coat," Donald said, "was like one of those long fancy sort of black coats that businessmen wear sometimes. The kinds that come down to their knees."

"Like an overcoat," Avery.

"Yeah," Donald said. "That's it."

Avery was running out of questions, feeling pretty certain that this interview with their only witness was a bust. She tried to find another relevant question as Ramirez stepped back into the room.

"I need to get going," Ramirez said. "Connelly wants me as an extra set of hands with some matter over near Boston College."

"That's fine," Avery said. "I think we're done here anyway."
She turned to Donald and said, "Mr. Greer, thank you so much for
your time."

Donald walked them out to the apartment building entrance and
waved them off as they got into the car.

"You tagging along with me?" Ramirez asked when they were
headed back down the street.

"No," she said. "I think I'm going to go back to the crime
scene."

"Kirkley Street?" he said.

"Yeah. You can take the car to do whatever errand Connelly
has you running. I'll catch a cab back to headquarters."

"You sure?"

"Yeah. It's not like I have anything else to—"

"To what?"

"Shit!"

"What is it?" Ramirez asked, concerned.

"Rose. I was supposed to hang out with Rose this afternoon. I
made this huge deal about a girls' day out. And it looks like that's
not going to happen. I'm going to have to let her down *again*."

"She'll understand," Ramirez said.

"No. No, she won't. I always do this to her."

Ramirez had no reply to that. The car remained in silence until
they reached Kirkley Street. Ramirez pulled the car to the side of
the street directly across from the morning's crime scene.

"Be careful," Ramirez said.

"I will," she said. She surprised herself when she leaned over
and kissed him briefly on the mouth.

She then got out of the car and started studying the scene
immediately. She was so focused and in the zone that she barely
noticed when Ramirez pulled away behind her.

CHAPTER SIX

After staring at the scene for a moment, Avery turned and looked down the street. Her eyes followed the path that Donald Greer must have been taking, all the way down to her right, where Kirkley intersected with Spring Street. She walked down the street, came to the intersection, and then turned.

Several thoughts entered her mind as she started to walk forward. Had the killer been on foot the entire time? And if so, why had he come in from Spring Street—a street just as barren and washed up as Kirkley? Or perhaps he had come by car. If that was the case, where would he have parked? If the fog had been thick enough, he could have parked anywhere along Kirkley and his car could have gone unseen.

If the man in the long black coat was indeed their killer, he had walked along this same route less than eight hours ago. She tried to envision the scene shrouded in thick morning fog. Because it was such a desolate area of town, it was not hard to do. As she walked slowly forward to the lot where the bones and the shards hard been found, she kept her eyes open for potential places the man could have ducked out of sight.

There were plenty of them, to be sure. There were six empty lots and two side streets that the man could have hidden in. If the fog had been thick enough, any of those locations would have made for ample cover.

That raised an interesting thought. If the man had hidden in one of those areas, he had let Donald Greer go by without bothering him. That took out the possibility of the murder being an act of sheer violence. Most people capable of that sort of violence would not have let Donald pass by so easily. In fact, Donald would have become a victim in most cases.

If she needed any further proof that the body had been burned somewhere else, this thought gave it to her. Perhaps, then, the item the man had been shifting beneath his coat had been a container holding the remains that he had dumped in the lot.

It made sense and she slowly started to feel a ramped-up sense of accomplishment. Now she was getting somewhere.

She walked to the lot where the remains had been found. Ever efficient and prompt, O'Malley had already cleared police away from the scene. She assumed he had done this just as soon as forensics had come by and collected the remains.

She walked to where the bones and ash had been dumped and simply stood there, looking around. The marshy area behind the lot was more visible than ever now. It was so close and much less open than the lot. So why would someone dump the bones in the middle of the lot rather than a weeded-over creek? Why would they put the remains right out in the open rather than ditching them in mud and stagnant water?

It was a question they had already approached. And in her mind, the answer was proof that they were dealing with a serial killer.

Because he wants people to see his work. He's proud and maybe a little arrogant.

She thought he might be clever, too. The use of fog to hide himself indicated that he had planned things very well. He'd have to be persistent about checking the weather to make sure there would be ample fog. He also had to know the area relatively well. It would have to have taken some serious planning.

And fire...he'd have to know fire well. To burn a body so cleanly without charring or otherwise damaging the bones spoke of dedication and patience. The killer would really have to know a great deal about fire and the process of burning.

Burning, she thought. *Fire.*

As she studied the crime scene and envisioned the killer standing in this same place, she felt like she was missing something—that some crucial clue was staring her right in the face. But all there was to see was the marshy and muddy area at the back of the property as well as the small square of space where some poor victim had been dumped out as if they were nothing more than a standard pile of trash.

She looked around the empty lot again and wondered if perhaps the location of the remains was not as important as she thought. If the killer was using fire as a way to send a message to someone (either the victim or the police), maybe *that* was what she needed to focus on.

With an idea coming to her mind, she pulled out her phone and called up the closest cab company for a ride out of there. After the call was placed and the cab had been requested, she looked through her contacts and stared at her daughter's name for five seconds.

I'm so sorry, Rose, she thought.

She pressed CALL and brought the phone to her ear as her heart broke a little.

Rose answered on the third ring. She sounded happy right away. Avery could hear music playing softly in the background.

She could imagine Rose getting ready for their afternoon out and hated herself a little.

"Hey, Mom," Avery said.

"Hey, Rose."

"What's up?"

"Rose…" she said. She felt tears coming on. She looked out at the empty lot behind her, trying to convince herself that she *had* to do this and that one day, Rose would understand.

Without Avery having to say another word, Rose apparently caught on to the emotion. She let out a little angry laugh. "Perfect," Rose said, the joy now gone from her voice. "Mom, are you fucking serious right now?"

Avery had heard Rose curse before but this time it was like a dagger to her heart because she deserved it.

"Rose, a case came up. A pretty bad one and I have to—"

"I know what you have to do," Rose said. She did not scream. She barely even raised her voice. And somehow, that made it that much worse.

"Rose, I can't help this. I certainly didn't expect this to pop up. When I made those plans with you, I had a wide open schedule for a few days. But this thing popped and…well, things change."

"I guess they do sometimes," Rose said. "But not with you. With you, things pretty much stay the same…when it comes to me, anyway."

"Rose, that's not fair."

"Don't you even *try* telling me what's not fair right now! And you know what, Mom? Just forget about it. This time and any other time you might want to pretend to play Good Mother in the future. It's not in the cards for us."

"Rose—"

"I get it, Mom. I do. But do you know how much it sucks to have this woman as your mother…a kick-ass woman with a demanding job? A woman I respect the hell out of…but a woman that time and time again disappoints me?"

Avery had no idea what to say. Which was just as well, since Rose was done.

"Bye, Mom. Thanks for letting me know in advance, though. Better than being stood up altogether, I guess."

"Rose, I—"

But the line went dead.

Avery shoved her phone back into her pocket and took a deep breath. A single tear rolled down her face from her right eye and she wiped it away as quickly as she could. She then walked purposefully over to the area that had been cordoned off with crime scene tape earlier in the morning and stared at it for a very long time.

Fire, she thought. *Maybe it's more than something the killer is using for his acts. Maybe it's symbolic. Maybe fire offers more of a clue than anything else.* So as she waited for the cab to arrive, she thought of fire and what sort of person might use it to deliver some sort of a message. It was hard to get a grasp on it, though, as she knew very little about arson.

I'll need a second mind at work on this, she thought.

And with that thought, she pulled out her phone and called up the A1 headquarters. She asked to be put through to Sloane Miller, the A1 psychologist and in-house shrink for the officers and detectives. If anyone could tap into the mind of a killer with fire on the brain, it would be Sloane.

CHAPTER SEVEN

Avery was back at A1 headquarters half an hour later. Upon entering, she did not take the elevator up to her office. Instead, she remained on the first floor and walked toward the back of the building. She'd been here before when she had been ordered to speak with Sloane Miller, the on-hand psychologist, during her last big and daunting case and it had affected her in a way she had still not quite come to terms with. But now she was visiting for another reason...for insight into a killer's mind. And, being in her element, the visit felt more natural.

She came to Sloane's office and was relieved to find the door cracked open. Sloane had no real set schedule and was more of a first-come-first-serve sort of resource for the police force. When Avery knocked on her door, she could hear Sloane typing something into her laptop.

"Come in," Sloane said.

Avery did, feeling much more at ease than the last time she'd met Sloane. Here in her office rather than her lobby-like setting for patients, things were a little more formal.

"Ah, Detective Black," Sloane said with genuine cheer as she looked up from her laptop. "It's so good to see you! I was very pleased to hear from you when you called. How have you been?"

"Things are good," Avery said. But in the back of her mind she knew that Sloane would jump at the opportunity to analyze her issues with Rose and her complicated relationship with Ramirez.

"What can I do for you today?" Sloane asked.

"Well, I was hoping to get your insights into a particular personality type. I'm leading up a case involving a man that we are fairly certain is burning his victims. He's left only bones and ash behind at the crime scene—cleaned bones, with no charring or damage. There's also a pile of ash and a slight chemical smell to the air...coming from the ash, I think. It's pretty clear he knows what he's doing. He knows how to burn a body, which seems like a very specific knowledge to have. But I don't think he's using the fire solely as a tool for his acts. I need to know what sort of person would not only use fire in such a way but also use it as some sort of symbolism."

"The idea that he's using the fire as a symbol of sorts is a great deduction," Sloane said. "In a case like this, I can almost guarantee you that's what's going on. At the heart of it, I think you might be dealing with someone that has an interest or maybe even a background in arson. Maybe he once had a job or hobby that included fire as a part of it. Studies have shown pretty resolutely that even children who are fascinated with campfires or matches show signs of an interest in arson-related acts."

"Can you tell me anything about that sort of personality that might help us get this guy sooner rather than later?"

"I can certainly try," Sloane said. "First of all, there's going be some sort of mental issues, but nothing too deep. It could just be something as simple as a tendency towards anger in even the most innocent of situations. He'll likely also be undereducated. Most repeat arsonists didn't graduate high school. Some see it as a way to rebel against a system they could never understand—the whole *some men just want to watch the world burn* nonsense. Some will claim they set fires as an act of revenge but can never define what it is they are seeking revenge against.

"They usually feel isolated or set apart from the world. So there's a good chance you're looking for either a single man or a man that is part of a loveless marriage. I'd expect he lives alone in a small house—probably spends a lot of time in a home office, basement, or garage of some kind."

"And what happens when you mix all of that with someone that clearly has no issue with killing people?"

"That does make it tricky," Sloane admitted. "But I think the same rules apply. Arsonists are usually very interested in people seeing what they've done. Setting fires is a way to attract attention. They're almost proud of it, like it's something they created. As for your suspect leaving the remains…that's a strange one. I suppose it could be linked to reports of arsonists visiting the scene of their fires to watch firemen put them out. The arsonist sees the firefighters working hard and feels that he made that happen—that the arsonist is, in a sense, controlling the firefighters."

"So do you think our suspect might be hanging out nearby, watching?"

Sloane considered it for a moment and then shrugged. "It's certainly a possibility. But the precision which you said he's burning the bodies—right down to clean bone—makes me think that this guy is also patient and organized. I don't think he'd so something as foolish as revisiting the scene of a crime."

Patient and organized, Avery thought. *That goes right along with his exquisite planning, using fog as cover to get his victims and dump the remains.*

She thought of the way the bones had been put almost on display—almost as jarring and as obvious as a raging fire.

"Do you have any opinions on the case yet?" Sloane asked.

"I'm thinking it's a serial killer. As far as we know, this is his first victim but the blatant way he displayed the remains irks me. More than that, there's something very organized about collecting a victim, burning them just right, and then dumping the remains in a specific manner. It screams serial tendencies to me."

"I'd agree with that," Sloane said.

"I just wish some of the men I work with were that bright," Avery said with a smirk.

"So how are *you* doing these days, Avery? No bullshit, please."

"I really am okay, all things considered. For the first time in my life, my problems seem sort of normal compared to my past."

"What sort of normal problems?" Sloane asked.

"Problems with my daughter. Relationship confusion with a guy."

"Ah, the perils of a hard-working woman."

Avery smiled, although she sensed a deeper conversation coming on. This was why she sighed internally when her phone rang at that exact moment. She dug it out of her pocket and saw Connelly's number. "I have to take this."

She nodded.

Avery stepped out of the office and answered the call in the hallway.

"Black, don't let this go to your head, but you were right. Dental records came back from the remains. You nailed it. The victim is Keisha Lawrence. Thirty-nine years old and lived within a mile of the area."

"What else do we know?" Avery said, looking past the compliments.

"Enough to ramp this thing up a bit," he said. "I've got some guys digging on this but right now we know for sure that she had no immediate family in the area. The only person of interest we have is a boyfriend and a mother that died pretty recently."

"Has anyone spoken with the boyfriend yet?"

"I've got someone on it right now. Meanwhile, I ran his background. This jack-off has a rap sheet of domestic abuse and bar fights. A real champ, this one."

"Want me to get to him after your current guy?"

"Yes…go talk to this creep next. I'll call Ramirez and get him off of the Boston College detail. He's all yours for the rest of the day."

Did she pick up a hint of sarcasm in his voice? She was pretty sure she had. Either that or she was getting paranoid.

Your sex life is not that important, she thought. *Get over yourself.*

"Haul ass, Black," Connelly said. "Let's get this guy before another pile of bones turns up."

Avery ended the call and hurried down to the parking garage for a car. She thought of what Sloane had said about arsonists often watching firemen at work, feeling that they were controlling the firemen in a way.

Maybe we need to add potential voyeur to the list of potential suspect characteristics, she thought.

As for arsonists wanting to feel that they were controlling the people working to understand his crimes…Avery Black was no fireman and she sure as hell didn't like feeling like someone was controlling her.

She pulled out of the parking garage quickly, the tires making a quick and satisfying shriek of traction as she sped out. Keisha Lawrence's boyfriend was their first real lead on this case and Avery wanted to pay him a visit before anyone else.

CHAPTER EIGHT

Avery parked in front of the boyfriend's apartment just as Ramirez was getting out of his own car in front of her. He gave her a smile that felt different than usual. Whether she wanted to admit it or not, they were bonding in a way that went much deeper than a simple partnership at work.

"How were things at the college?" Avery asked as they met at the stairs to the house.

"Stuffy. Some stupid protest-related thing. So what's the deal here?"

"Boyfriend with an aggressive past. Pretty rough abuse-related rap sheet. I got a call on the way over that says he was almost confrontational with the police who broke the news."

"So fun times ahead, huh?" Ramirez asked.

Avery nodded as they started up the stairs. She buzzed the doorbell and listened to heavy footsteps approaching the door. Within seconds, a slightly heavyset man answered the door. He was thick in the gut, but shoulders and arms that had clearly seen some time in the gym stood out from the tank top he wore. Both arms were decorated with several tattoos, one of which was a naked woman straddling a skull.

"Yeah?" he said, sounding more irritated than sad.

"Are you Adam Wentz?" Avery asked.

"Who's asking?"

Avery flashed her badge and said, "I'm Detective Black and this is Detective Ramirez. We'd like to ask you some questions about Keisha."

"I've talked about her enough today," Adam Wentz said. "Having two policemen come to your house early in the morning to tell you that a woman you're seeing is dead is a hell of a way to start your day. So I'm done talking about it."

"Forgive me for saying so," Avery said, "but I'd expect a man who had just lost his girlfriend in such a tragic way would want to help in any way he could while the police try to get to the bottom of it all."

"No matter what you find, it won't bring her back now, will it?" Adam said.

"No, it won't," Avery said. "But any information you can give us might help find the man that did it."

Adam rolled his eyes. "So am I supposed to invite you in and weep on the couch about how much I miss her and how badly I want the killer brought to justice? Some shit like that?"

"Would that be so bad?" Ramirez asked.

With that, Adam stepped out of the doorway, closed the door behind him, and stood on the front stoop. It was clear that Avery and Ramirez were not going to be invited inside.

"I'm really not in the mood for this," Adam said. "So let's make it quick. What do you want?"

Avery took a moment to try to figure out his hostile attitude. Was it some sort of weird way to express his grief? Was he hiding something? It was too early to know for sure.

He either knows something or was more hurt by the news than he expected, she thought. *We have to be careful with our questions here.*

"For right now," Avery said, "we're just trying to narrow down our options and figure out a timeline."

Adam crossed his arms and gave a quick and gruff "All right."

"Can you provide a timeline of where you were over the course of the past two days?" Avery asked.

"I went to work yesterday and the day before. Clocked in at eight, clocked out at five thirty both times. I came home, had a sandwich and a few beers for dinner. A very exciting life, as you can see."

"Did you see Keisha during any of that time?" Avery asked.

"Yeah. She came over around seven the night before last. We watched some TV and then had sex on the couch."

Avery felt anger flaring up in her—that a man like Adam Wentz could speak about his recently deceased girlfriend in such an offhanded way placed a drop of acid in her stomach. Behind her, she sensed Ramirez taking a step closer. She knew from working with him that he wasn't taking well to Adam's mood, either.

"Did she sleep over?" Avery asked.

"No. She hasn't slept here in a while. She says it makes her late for work."

"It doesn't have anything to do with your history of abusing women?" Ramirez asked.

Avery cringed, not liking that Ramirez had taken the conversation in that direction. Adam looked directly at him, totally unthreatened, and scowled.

"No, actually," Adam said. "It's because her apartment is about twenty minutes closer to her work, you prick."

Ramirez stepped closer, now standing beside Avery and about three feet away from Adam.

"What did you do after she left two nights ago?" Avery asked.

"I went to bed, just like I did last night," Adam said. "Woke up this morning and started getting ready for work. That's when I got the call that Keisha had died. Your two cop friends were over about half an hour later."

"How did you feel when getting the news?" Avery asked.

"What kind of stupid question is that?"

Ramirez stepped up one more time, now on the stairs. He glared up at Adam with far too much contempt in his gaze for Avery's liking. "Can you just answer the question?" Ramirez asked.

"I was surprised," Adam said. "A little sad, I guess. Yeah, she was *sort of* my girlfriend but it wasn't too serious."

"How long had you dated?" Avery asked.

"About seven months. We weren't committed or anything."

"And is there any way you can prove you were at home last night? Maybe you went online at some point and we could check your internet history. Something like that?"

"No, and I don't...wait...are you actually thinking I did this? You think I killed her?"

"No, I didn't say that," Avery said. "I'm just trying to establish where you were when we believe she was killed. Trust me...I would love nothing more than for you to provide a reason to eliminate you from the equation."

"Well, I can't prove when I was sleeping, now can I? And I don't know why in the hell you'd think I did it anyway."

"Sir," Ramirez said, trying his best to remain civil. "We just have to go on what we have. And your history really leaves us no choice *but* to question you."

"Look, I only hit Keisha once. *Ever.* I'm not one of those losers that gets off on beating women."

"Your record says otherwise," Ramirez said.

"Drop it, Ramirez," Avery said.

I don't know if he's being protective over me or just showing off, but this could get pretty bad if he doesn't check himself.

"Yeah, listen to the pretty lady," Adam said.

"You don't know when to shut your mouth, do you?" Ramirez asked. He surged forward, reaching for his cuffs. "If you'd kept your mouth shut, I wouldn't have to arrest you."

"Arrest me?" Adam said. "For what?"

Ramirez didn't bother with an answer. He grabbed Adam by the shoulder and tried to spin him around, pulling his arm back to cuff him. Adam, however, wasn't having it. He jerked away and held his hand out—not pushing Ramirez, but keeping him at bay.

"Get your hand off of me," Ramirez said as calmly as he could.

40

"You're not arresting me," Adam said. "I didn't do anything."

"You've been hostile and rude from the moment you answered your door."

"My girlfriend just died...burned right the fuck up! Of course I've been rude!"

"Oh, now you care about her dying?"

Adam gave a slight shove then, nearly making Ramirez fall down the stairs. Avery saw the look on Adam's face; he knew he had messed up with that one action. Ramirez responded by quickly squatting and launching himself into Adam. Both men stumbled backward and slammed into the closed front door.

Avery would have handled things totally differently but she saw where Ramirez was coming from. The guy *did* seem shady. She didn't think he was the killer, but he was certainly worth looking into...only not like this.

By the time she had dashed up the few steps and to the small stoop of a porch, Ramirez had Adam Wentz pushed face-first against the door and was slapping his cuffs on him.

"You're under arrest," Ramirez said.

"For what?" Adam asked, his face still pressed against the door.

"I'll have to check the books for the proper terminology for *being an asshole,*" Ramirez said. "Accosting an officer won't look good, either."

Avery stepped back for a moment as Ramirez led Adam Wentz down the stairs and to the car. Adam did not put up a fight. Avery wondered if this was some sort of resigned defeat on his part or just being smart and making sure he didn't get himself into any further trouble. She watched as Ramirez shut the door on Wentz and then opened his own door to get in.

Avery stood at the hood of the car and nodded him over. "Come here," she said.

"Yeah?" he asked, closing the door and meeting her in front of the car.

"You could have handled that better," she said. "This was an unnecessary arrest."

"You don't think he's guilty?"

"I don't. He's certainly worth further questioning, but not worthy of what just happened. If he's a smart man—and that's probably a stretch, let's be honest—he could go after you with a lawyer."

"Are you...what? Are you upset about this?"

"A little."

"He was being really rude and inappropriate with you."

"I've had tons of people be rude and inappropriate to me in this line of work," Avery countered. "This is no different. I have to wonder if you might not have cared quite as much if we weren't sleeping together."

He looked offended at first but then grinned at her. She was a bit disarmed by it because, even in the midst of her frustration with him, it was damned sexy.

"Maybe I wouldn't have," he said. "But it's done now. Let's take him back to the A1 and see what we can get out of him."

Without allowing her time for a response, he went got into the car on the passenger side. Avery looked into the back of the car and saw that Wentz's face was like a stone—perfectly still and cold.

With an uneasy feeling in her stomach, Avery got behind the wheel and took Adam Wentz to A1 headquarters.

CHAPTER NINE

Half an hour later, Avery looked at Adam Wentz through a two-way mirror. Ramirez was with her, as were Connelly and O'Malley. O'Malley was reading through Wentz's file, grumbling a few words here and there.

"If this cretin is smart enough to kidnap and then burn the body of someone, then I'll do a little dance on a bar tabletop right now," he said. "This guy's a waste of space. Yeah, he likely deserves to be in jail for *some* reason, but not for the death of Keisha Lawrence."

"We can't know that for certain," Connelly said. "Not until we've properly questioned him."

"Yeah, good luck with that," Ramirez said. "It's like talking to a brick wall…a very badly tattooed brick wall."

Connelly and O'Malley both looked at Avery. She shrugged and looked back out at Wentz. "I can give it a try, I suppose."

"And do it without Ramirez this time," O'Malley said. "The only thing Wentz has said since we sat him down in there was that Ramirez was too rough with him and arrested him on a bullshit charge. Which is *technically* true. But I can figure things out on that end. We can keep him here for a while."

"I don't think we need to," Avery said. "It's not our guy."

"How about you question him before you jump to such a conclusion?" O'Malley said.

Avery sighed and left the room. Before she entered the interrogation room, she took a moment to collect herself. She hated to play the sexism card but she felt pretty sure that the men in the room she had just left might think more of her opinion if she had a penis. It was a nice daydream to think that the workplace had evolved beyond such things but at the end of the day, Avery was well aware of the lay of the land.

Wentz will likely see me the same way, she thought. *Got to make sure I don't give him a reason to.*

She stepped into the interrogation room and closed the door behind her. She wasn't going to play good cop and she wasn't going to play bad cop. She was going to question him like a good little detective and provide enough proof to the men behind the mirror so they could let Wentz go—and so she could get back on the trail of the real killer. If she needed to, she'd get a little forceful but she didn't think it would come to that if she played her cards right.

She took the seat on the other side of the small table he was sitting at, ignoring the hateful look on Adam's face.

43

"What sort of relationship did you have with Keisha?" Avery asked. "You've said it wasn't a fully committed relationship and you've also insinuated that there was sex involved. Would you say you were emotionally attached to her?"

Adam thought about this for a moment with a lopsided smile on his face. "Honestly...no," he finally answered. "I liked hanging out with her and the sex stuff was really good. But we never lied to each other about what we had, you know? I saw other people and so did she."

"There *is* a report in your file from about four months ago where she reported you beating her," Avery said. "She later dropped it. Why is that? Did you threaten her?"

"No. We got into an argument and I slapped her. Pretty hard."

"Do you recall what the argument was about?"

"Over the stupid dog," he said. "I hate that dog. She'd bring it over to my place and it always jumped up on the couch. It would beg me to pet it. She brought it over one time when she wasn't feeling well and asked me if I'd walk it. I refused and the damn thing ended up pissing on my carpet. So I kicked the dog. And she got upset. We got into an argument, some things were said, and I ended up slapping her."

"And what about the other reports of abuse on your report? There are two others and they both come from the same woman."

"My ex-wife. Yeah..."

"Mr. Wentz, I want you to understand that I am not trying to rub your nose in your past. I am simply doing everything I can to help prove that you did not do this. And you have to understand that the way you responded to my partner and I makes things seem a little suspicious."

Adam looked down at the table. Avery noticed his eyes shifting to the left and right. There also seemed to be a relaxed sort of posture to his shoulders, whereas he had been rigid and upright when she had first come in. These were all signs of a sort of resignation—that he was slowly dropping his tough-guy routine.

"I had to go to court for one of the times with my wife," he said. "I got drunk, she complained about it, and I responded by pushing her to the ground. When she came charging after me, I stopped her with my fist."

"Is that why she left you?"

Adam smirked and shook his head. "No. I left her. She wanted kids and I didn't. She'd try to make me feel guilty about it, so I left her. But what does that have to do with Kcisha, anyway?"

"Nothing," Avery said. "So back to Keisha then. Did you know her well enough to know what the routine of her days was like?"

"Yeah, I guess so."

"Walk me through a typical day for her, would you? As well as you can."

He shook his head in disbelief, clearly finding this whole line of questioning over the top. "Her day starts with the damn dog. Walks it every morning right when she wakes up, even before breakfast. She works from home as an editor for some sort of proposal center or something. She doesn't really get out too much. Other than coming to my place and maybe a bar every now and again, she was a recluse, you know?"

"When she walked her dog, do you know if there was any regular route she'd take?"

"No clue. Whenever she started talking about the dog, I sort of tuned out."

"When you spoke to her on that last night before she left your apartment, were things on good terms?"

"Yeah. Things *have* been on good terms for a while now. We've had a pretty good month. Well...*had*, I guess."

"And I guess if she didn't get out often, she really didn't make many enemies, did she?"

"None that I know of."

Avery nodded and drummed her fingers on the table. "Can I ask you something a little personal?"

"Why not? It's not like you're *not* going to ask it anyway, right?"

Ignoring his stubbornness, Avery went on. "Why is it that you *don't* seem too upset? You do understand why someone might find that suspicious, right?"

"Yeah, I do. And you know what, maybe I did cry a little when I got that call. But there's something about the way she was killed...I don't know. It makes it almost unreal. It's so obscene, you know?"

As he said this, he looked dismissively to the table again. Avery was certain that he had worked on his tough-guy persona over the years and that it was finally breaking down in a moment of vulnerability.

Maybe that's why he is coming off as so emotionless during this while ordeal.

"Yes, I think I could understand that," Avery said. "From here, I'm afraid we'll have to reach out to your employer to ask them some questions. Very basic stuff, just to help the investigation along."

"Do whatever," he said, again looking at the table.

She wanted to apologize to him for the way he had been brought in but also knew that if she *had* caused him to break a bit and discover his grief, he needed to be left alone.

She left the room and reentered the observation room. O'Malley and Connelly were looking at her with confused expressions. Ramirez smiled at her but didn't seem to know how to feel.

"That's it?" O'Malley asked.

"That's it. He's not our guy."

"How can you be so sure?" Connelly asked.

"Several reasons. If he was the killer, he would have admitted it to it by now—or, at the very least, been covert about dropping clues. Someone that kills people the way our guy is doing it wants the attention. More than that, Adam Wentz doesn't fit the profile. He's not motivated enough. A domestic abuse charge on his record does not equate to murderer-who-burns-his-victims."

She could see that her explanation was getting through to them. But she knew Connelly well enough. He'd try to hold on to Wentz for as long as he could…just to have someone sitting in the A1 as a suspect while a hunt was underway for the real killer. It was his way of feeling productive.

"You're sure?" O'Malley asked.

"Almost positive. I was right about the identity of the remains we found, right? Why's it so hard to believe I'm right about this? And not only this, but also that we likely have a serial killer on our hands?"

The two superiors exchanged a confounded look which ended with a frustrated smile on O'Malley's face.

"All right, Black," Connelly said. "I'm going to keep Wentz here for a while longer to see if he offers up anything new."

"He won't," she said.

Ignoring her, Connelly added: "In the meantime, why don't you and Ramirez get out there and prove yourself right. Again."

"Gladly," she said.

She glanced through the window again and was not at all surprised to see Adam Wentz with his head in his hands, doing his best to hide the fact that he was finally crying.

CHAPTER TEN

The day rounded out with no leads and no new clues and, as such, led Avery to the A1's bar of choice later that afternoon, Joe's Pub. She took her usual spot at the bar with Ramirez beside her. A few other cops were with them, drinking beer and watching the Red Sox lose on the TV mounted behind the bar. As was the norm, the little cluster of cops had their own little part of the bar along the far side of the building. It was there that they gathered to talk about current cases and let out their frustrations over beer, darts, and watching the Red Sox or Patriots on TV.

Avery sat there and looked back on her day, seeing if she could dig out any missing pieces from everything that had occurred. She and Ramirez had worked with the guys in Forensics to go over the ashes and the remains but no matter how they looked at it, they had no new information. Avery knew that cases like this usually took some time to come together but still felt as if she was failing. And it had been that looming sense of failure that led her to the bar. She did not drink to drown her sorrows and failures, but to sort them out and find a way to change them.

She wished she could just zone out and enjoy the baseball game on TV or a game of darts in the back of the bar, but she didn't quite work that way, though. While she was well aware of the chatter from her co-workers all around, she remained deep in thought. She was trying to figure out the sort of man who had the patience, the experience, and the twisted mind it took to kidnap someone, burn them, and dump their remains in a public area. She wondered if the location had some significance. She wondered, albeit briefly, if the empty lot was where the killer had abducted Keisha Lawrence. The lot itself hadn't been too far away from her apartment. And if she had been walking her dog when she went missing—

These recycled and rehashed thoughts tapered off as she heard one of the nearby officers mention a name that grabbed her interest.

"Did you hear that Desoto is getting out early?" one of the cops said.

"Bullshit," replied the other. "How?"

"Good behavior, if you can believe it."

"Unreal. We're talking, what…almost a full year?"

"Something like that."

"Someone is pulling some strings somewhere," came the reply.

47

Avery knew the name Desoto well. After all, she had managed to take him down, along with four of his best men. It was one of the cases that had made Avery something of a figurehead around the A1. Desoto was the head of at least two gangs—maybe more—and had gained such a boogeyman status that a lot of people had not even believed he really existed—not until Avery had brought him in. And now that there was a chance he was getting out early...

That's another little treat to look forward to, she thought. *He'll be looking for revenge right away when he steps foot out of prison.*

"You good?" Ramirez asked her, gently nudging her arm.

She blinked her thoughts away and nodded. "Yeah, I'm good," she said, taking a sip from her beer.

"You really don't feel good about Adam Wentz, do you? You really don't think he's our guy?"

"No, I don't. And I think it's almost criminal to hold him."

"Yeah, but even if he isn't our guy, he might know something, right?"

"I doubt it. He would have told me when he started to crack. He was crying like a baby when I left that room."

"So tell me this: if we did find out it was him and tomorrow this case is closed, would you be okay being wrong?"

She thought about it for a moment and then shook her head. "No. It's never okay to be wrong. But in this case, there's no worry. I'm not wrong."

He sighed and then chuckled. He ordered another beer as one of his work-buddies came over. His name was Eldridge and although he was a damned good cop, he was also something of a frat boy at heart. Finley, who had become a good friend to Avery over the last few months, was shadowing him.

"You guys having a love spat or something?" Eldridge asked.

"Hardly," Avery said.

"I know sexual tension when I see it," Eldridge said. "I can say this with full confidence because the tension stage is about as far as I ever get."

"A stand-up specimen like yourself?" Avery asked sarcastically. "I don't believe it."

"What are you two doing here anyway?" Finley asked. "A long day of work, I think a better reward than a beer would be some stress-sex."

Avery decided not to say anything else. She didn't know if they were insinuating something or if they knew about them somehow. She and Ramirez had been teased about a sexual relationship before, but never as bad as they had been over the last day.

48

Apparently picking up on Avery's shift in mood, Ramirez recovered for them both. "If you two think she'd sleep with me in the first place, you're shitty cops. She's got standards, man."

Eldridge and Finley laughed at this and after some further goodhearted ribbing, they got their drinks and headed back to their end of the bar.

"Sorry about that," Ramirez said. "Look...I haven't told anyone."

"I didn't say you had."

"Maybe it's just the afterglow," he joked. "Maybe the sex is so good, we have an aura about us or something."

"Getting cocky now, are we?" she said, her voice low.

"Are you kidding? I slept with you last night *and* woke up with you this morning. So yeah...I'm feeling a little arrogant."

She smiled at him and a large part of her thought Eldridge might have been right. Maybe she *would* rather be in a bed with Ramirez than in a bar. On the other hand, if they left together that would only add more fuel to the fire. And she hated to be in the spotlight...especially over something like this.

"They might be on to something, though," Ramirez said. "You want to get out of here?"

"I am after this beer," Avery said. "But I'm going home alone."

"You sure?" he said.

"Yeah," she said. "And that's nothing against you...I just need to try to get ahead on this case."

He nodded and smirked. "That's one of the reasons I like you, Avery."

She finished her beer and returned his smirk. "Careful," she said. "With talk like that, people might start to think there's something going on between us."

***

When she was in her apartment with the case files spread out around her, she knew she'd made the right decision. And she was pretty sure Ramirez knew her well enough to know that she had, too. She looked over the notes that Forensics had mocked up and although they made little sense to her, she knew enough about them to know that there were no answers there to be had.

The one thing of note they had managed to come up with was that there *was* a chemical present in the ashes but it was so disintegrated that it was hard to make out what it was. It could have been anything from basic rubbing alcohol to a toxic agent.

49

Probably some kind of burning accelerant, she thought. *Could be something as simple as gas or kerosene.*

Midnight crept up on her faster than she'd expected. When she turned out the lights and readied herself for bed, she thought it would be nice to have Ramirez there. She nearly called him but did not want to seem needy. In fact, she wasn't needy at all. What had happened the night before had been nice but she did not want him to think that she *needed* it. She had never needed a man in order to feel complete and she wasn't about to start now. Yes, she supposed she cared for Ramirez, but was she ready to settle down and commit herself to a relationship?

That was a stretch...

She lay in bed for fifteen minutes before she realized that sleep was not going to come as quickly as she hoped. There was just too much on her mind. The case, Ramirez and the complications he brought with him, and, perhaps most burdensome, Rose.

Thinking of Rose, Avery sat up in bed and flipped on her bedside lamp. It was too late to call her, but maybe a text that she'd get in the morning would be okay.

Avery considered it for a moment but then decided not to. Instead, she opened up Facebook. Sadly, Facebook had been her only reliable outlet over the last year to see how her daughter's life was going.

She pulled up Rose's page and saw that she had been blocked.

She knew it should be a silly offense at most, but it actually hurt her. She checked Instagram and Twitter as well but she was blocked there, too. Apparently, her backing out of their girls' day had been the last straw.

The hell of it was that Avery didn't blame her. She'd just have to figure out a way to make it up to her—if Rose would even let her try, of course. And at this point, there was no guarantee that she would.

She sadly set her phone down and tried to drift off to sleep. When she finally did, it was a fitful sleep. There was no real rest, just a frantic mind trying to relax while also sorting through the chaos that its owner's life had become.

***

She knew it was a nightmare right from the start, but that did nothing to make it any less horrific. She was walking through the lot where they had discovered the remains. There was a new pile of bones there, only these weren't as cleanly stripped and pearly white

50

as they had been in real life. Meat still clung to these bones. Flies buzzed almost comically around them.

From the back of the property, where the marshy ground began, Rose came walking toward her.

"Messy, huh?" Rose said.

"Did you see it?" Avery asked. "Did you see it happen?"

"I don't see much these days," Rose said. "Especially not of you. But maybe this will help."

With that, Rose pulled a lighter from her pocket, flicked the flame to life, and threw it at Avery. Avery was alight at once, her pants catching on fire. The flames blazed upward instantly, charring her shirt and the underside of her chin.

She screamed. From behind her, she heard Ramirez calling her name. She turned to him and saw that he was there with an arm outstretched and a blanket like the fire department often carried into fires to put out burning victims.

"Just take my hand," Ramirez said. "I can save you. You just have to trust me."

And although she badly wanted to, she did not reach out. In response, Ramirez screamed her name.

Avery fell to the ground, the flames now catching her arms and hair. She burned quickly, her skin like wax as she fell to the ground. She did not writhe, but merely lay there and looked back at Rose.

Rose held a stick with a marshmallow at the end of it. She hunkered down on the ground and held it over her flaming mother.

"I'll take the quality time however I can," Rose said with a laugh.

It was then that Avery finally screamed. Flames erupted from her mouth as her entire body went up in a flash of ash, smoke, and intense white light.

Avery jerked awake in bed, the dream-scream locked in her throat and dangerously close to springing forth into the land of the waking.

It took her a few moments to realize that she was awake and that she had been pulled from sleep by the ringing of her phone. She reached for it with her heart hammering in her chest and saw that it was 5:15—thirty minutes before her morning alarm usually woke her. On the caller display screen, she saw Connelly's name and number.

"Yeah?" she said as she answered it.

"Get up, Black," he said. "We've got another body."

CHAPTER ELEVEN

When Avery pulled her car into the dusty and vacant lot behind what had once been a flour mill, something about the scene instantly jarred her. Faded white letters along the front of the building had once said STATLER BROTHERS FLOUR but the letters were barely visible now. She wondered how long ago this place had last seen a work day. Easily fifty years, she guessed. It was nothing unique, really. Nothing on this side of town had seen much activity in a very long time. These were more than the outskirts of Boston—this was just on the edge of the Mattapan area, a place that at times felt like some weird borderland that time had forgotten.

When she stepped out into the lot and headed over to the gathered policemen at the edge of the back lot, she could actually smell the neglect of the place. These were the sorts of places that were perfect for young experimental couples to explore the back seats of cars or for drug dealers to peddle their wares. But it felt different here for some reason…it felt *wrong* to display the end of one's life in such a forgotten place.

When she reached the gathered group at the edge of the lot, one of the policemen was finishing putting up the crime scene tape. There were only three others, one of whom was Connelly. Finley was also there looking excited yet a little hesitant as usual. He had a pale look on his face as he took in the scene beyond the crime scene tape.

Avery joined them, ducking under the crime scene tape and hunkering down about six inches from what the tape was blocking off.

It was another pile of remains—more bones and ashes. Only this time, there seemed to be much more ashes and fewer bones than before. The skull was the easiest to pinpoint. Avery also saw a femur, a few ribs, and what looked like a fractured wrist. She leaned down closer, inhaled deeply, and found that she could catch traces of the chemical smell that had been detected at the last crime scene.

What the hell is *that? Pretty sure it's not something common or basic. Maybe he's having to special order an accelerant from somewhere. If so, that could be potentially easy to trace.*

"How did we find this?" she asked.

"Some guy on the highway department turned around back here about two hours ago," Connelly said. "He said he only saw it because he got out of his truck to take a leak."

"So we have no idea how long these remains have been here?" Avery asked.

"Nope."

Avery scanned the rest of the area. The ashes and bones were in a fairly tidy pile like the previous crime scene. That led her to believe that everything else about this scene would also be identical to the previous one. The first indication of this was the several shards of what looked like broken porcelain or colored glass about five feet away from the ash.

"Looks just about the same as the shards from the last site," Avery pointed out.

"I noticed that," Connelly said.

As she was about to duck back under the crime scene tape and have a look around the area, she watched as two police cars came barreling into the lot. Their flashers were on but their sirens were silent. The lead car came to a screeching halt and the driver wasted no time in getting out.

"You guys from the A1?" the cop asked as he hurried over to them.

"Yeah," Connelly said. "Why?"

"Well, this is about a mile or so outside of your jurisdiction," the cop said. It was clear that he was irritated; there was an edge of annoyance to his voice. "This is a B3 matter. While we appreciate the interest and help, we can handle it from here."

"I'm sure you can," Connelly said. "But this scene is an exact replica of one we found yesterday. It's highly relevant to our case."

"But this is our turf," the cop argued. "This is—"

"Really?" Avery asked. "Your *turf*? This isn't some gang war. We've got two bodies so far...and no rhyme or reason to the attacks. If you want to talk about people stepping on your *turf*, take it up with your captain. We're too busy trying to catch a killer to worry about if we might be infringing on someone's turf."

"You better believe I'll take it to my captain," the cop said.

"You do that," Connelly said. "And by the time the right calls are made and the forms are filled out and filed, we'll be done here."

"Asshole," the cop said.

"Oh, I've been called much worse," Connelly said.

"You can't just take over a crime scene when it's outside of your jurisdiction!"

"We can if it's directly linked to a murder that was in our backyard. If anything, you and your boys should be gladly assisting."

"This is our jurisdiction," the B3 cop said. "*You'll* be doing the assisting."

"Yeah, that's not going to happen," Connelly said.

Avery could tell that he was starting to get ruffled. If O'Malley were also here, he might have been a little more aggressive. *Then again,* Avery thought, *if it gets any more aggressive, this could turn out very bad.*

"You really want to make this an issue?" the B3 cop asked.

"We were here first," Connelly said. "It seems to me that *you're* making this an issue."

"Damn it! My captain is going to hear about this!"

"You already said that. Now stop threatening me and let us work here, would you?"

The cop looked to Connelly for a moment, as if trying to think of a rebuttal. When it was clear he had no interest in starting a district versus district fight before going through the proper channels, he retreated back to his car. He kicked up dust and squealed tires out on the road as he left.

"So that's going to be a mess if he actually complains about this," Connelly said. "He's actually more right than wrong…so let's do our work quickly."

Avery wasted no time. She started scouring the area and took note as other cars appeared. Forensics worked quickly and efficiently once they arrived, bagging up the remains and the porcelain shards, taking measurements of the area, and so on. Avery walked along beside them, looking for any additional clues the killer might have left behind.

If he did leave clues, I don't know that they'd be accidental, she thought. *It could be another way of him showing off. But if he messed up and left a footprint, a thread, a hair, or some other damning evidence and we miss it because we're so thrown off by the nature of his crime, that could be bad.*

She looked around the immediate area bordering the crime scene tape and found nothing. *The guy moves like a ghost…which means he's careful and fast. The amount of planning he's doing is borderline obsessive.*

Done with the immediate area around the crime scene tape, Avery made her way to the farthest edge of the lot. It was separated from the one-way street that ran alongside the building by a tall brick wall. She walked along this wall, looking for any sort of accidental evidence such as stray fibers, but found nothing. She then checked the other side of the wall, but other than scattered litter, there was nothing to be found there, either.

She then turned her attention to the old flour mill. Just about every window was broken and it was covered in graffiti. There was a large door along the back that was halfway open. It looked to be an old loading door, permanently frozen in a partially open position. She walked up a set of crumbling concrete stairs and slipped inside.

Morning sunlight came in through the broken windows, casting an almost ethereal glow to the place. Dust motes drifted here and there, floating up to toward the high ceiling. The place was nothing more than old posts and a single large machine in the far back of the building. It was all one large room, littered with old broken equipment, rotted pallet boards, and dust.

That's why it was so easy for her to spot the earring on the floor. The fact that the dusty sunlight was reflecting from it made it that much easier. She walked over to it and could tell right away that it had not been here for very long. Unlike everything else around here, it was not coated in dust. The small diamond in the earring still had its luster and shine.

She heard footsteps approaching, coming up the concrete stairs outside. She looked to the loading door and watched as Ramirez walked in. He took a moment to observe the interior of the place and then looked down at her.

"Good morning, beautiful," he said.

"Good morning," she said. "Hey, can you run out and get someone from Forensics in here? I have something I need them to pick up."

Ramirez nearly seemed disappointed by her quick transition from flirtatious to professional but nodded anyway. She took no time to think about his reaction; she was looking at the floor, noticing yet another sign of recent activity.

She saw her own footprints, treading across the dusty floor. But she also saw another series of prints…and then another. There were no *clear* prints, but many scuffed ones, indicating that someone had been moving with urgency. One of the pairs of footprints—the smaller ones—looked as if they were being dragged.

The larger set gave her about three whole prints to go from. It was likely a boot of some kind. A work boot. Around a size eleven or twelve if her guess was correct. The other was a flat-soled sneaker of some kind. Avery thought she saw part of a star in a pattern of tread. It reminded her of the Converse All-Star symbol.

Probably a younger person, then. No older than early twenties.

There had been an altercation here. And while the prints were not brand new, they had certainly not been here for very long. A few days at most.

As she got to her feet and trailed the course of the prints, she saw the earring was directly in the path of the footprints. A woman had been attacked. She had been wearing sneakers, maybe All-Stars, and the man in pursuit had likely been wearing boots.

She stepped back and traced the course of the tracks with her eyes. She tried to picture the chase and struggle. The strides of the prints made her think there had been an element of surprise to the attack.

One of them was in here already when the other arrived. The faintness of the maybe-Converse prints makes it seem like that person was in a hurry, running. So the younger one was running away—probably surprised and terrified. The remains outside probably belong to this person.

Ramirez came back inside with a member of Forensics, breaking her train of thought. "What do we have here?" the Forensics member asked.

"An earring and some pretty telltale footprints."

"Goldmine," Ramirez said. "Nice work."

Avery nodded her thanks but was too preoccupied with the prints to pay much attention to him. There was no blood, nor any visible remains. They might be able to get DNA results from the earring post but that was a stretch.

But even that didn't bother Avery as much as the trail of footprints in the dust.

While there was no blood or visible signs of violence, those prints told a story that she did not like at all.

CHAPTER TWELVE

The day felt weighed down by the discovery they'd made in the morning. By the time four o'clock came around and results had started to pile in, Avery felt like she was wearing a set of lead weights around her shoulders. It was a weight she felt as she walked into the A1 conference room, growing heavier with every set of eyes that fell on her.

As she took a seat across from Ramirez, she noticed the stir of energy in the air. She knew that bits and pieces of information had been coming in (mostly things being ruled out by Forensics) and that the earring had been confirmed as belonging to an expensive set. Other than that, though, Avery had heard nothing concrete. The hushed whispers around the table and the fact that O'Malley was running late made her pretty sure that there'd be plenty to go over in the coming minutes.

She also knew that there was some nastiness going on behind the scenes. The A1 higher-ups were having some very heated conversations with the B3 brass. While she was not interested in the politics of it all, she knew that if things didn't get settled in a civil way very soon, they were going to have a logistical nightmare on their hands that might hinder the case.

At exactly 4:07, the room was filled with nine officers and the growing volume of rumors. Someone speculated that local media had caught wind of the story and would be talking about it on the evening news. Someone else speculated that the value of the earring suggested the killings were financially motivated, as the earrings were valued at about five hundred dollars.

When O'Malley arrived and finally entered the room, all whispers and rumors fell flat. O'Malley looked anxious and maybe even a little flustered—two words that Avery would have never used to describe him before this afternoon. He held a thin stack of papers in his right hand and his cell phone in his left. When he entered the room, he shut the door a bit too hard. The slamming noise made a few of the officers in the room jump.

"Welcome to one hell of a mess, everyone," he said as he stood at the front of the conference table. He instantly selected two stapled sheets of paper from his pile and slid them across the table to Avery.

Avery looked at the paper and was impressed at how quickly Forensics had gotten results. The paper in her hands identified the victim as Sarah Osborne, twenty-two years old.

"That name ring a bell?" O'Malley asked, nodding to the paper.

"The last name does," Avery said.

"Sarah Osborne," O'Malley said. "Niece of City Councilman Ron Osborne. The earring was confirmed as being hers exactly ten minutes ago. Turns out she also frequently wore Converse All-Stars."

A pair of Converses and five-hundred-dollar earrings, Avery thought. *This was a young lady who was still struggling to find her identity.*

"We've already got more news crews on this now," O'Malley continued. "Given the nature of the killings and the high profile of this victim, we can expect tons of media attention. And that means I'd like to wrap it up before it hits national headlines, especially with the B3 bitching about it. So someone...please tell me we're making some headway."

"There are no obvious connections between the victims," Avery said, still skimming the report on Sarah Osborne. "They lived in different parts of town and were from different financial backgrounds. I'm currently looking over the records for all traces of arson over the last ten years. It's slow going, but there are no links yet."

"I'll get three others to help with that," O'Malley said. "Meanwhile, let it be known that some of the guys from over at the B3 district are going to be working with us on this case. The newest body was on their grounds and seeing as how the victim had some notoriety about her, they're insisting on staying involved. I'm not a fan of this but it's just not worth the argument or media attention."

"Another thing," Avery said. "I think it's now safe to say that this *is* a serial killer. If you want this wrapped quickly, I think we need to consider bringing the FBI in."

"And in addition to the arson," Connelly said from his place at the table, "I think we should also cross-reference any records from former law enforcement. Maybe even Forensics, specifically. This guy cleans up after himself a little too well. It's almost like he knows the sort of things we would be looking for."

Avery bit back the comment that came to her tongue. She felt it was a good thought but was pretty sure Connelly's cross-reference suggestion would be a waste of time. Fire was the key. She was almost certain of it now...she just had to find solid proof.

"For now, that's all we've got," O'Malley said. "If any of you speaks to the media, I'll have your ass. I give it about another two or three hours before we have vans and reporters lined up outside. So keep your head down, your nose clean, and your mouth shut.

Finley, Smith, and Cho…I want you three working on the cross-references Black and Connelly discussed. Black and Ramirez, I'm going to need you to visit the Osborne family."

"When were they told about Sarah's death?" Avery asked.

"About an hour ago. If you're lucky, you'll get to speak with the parents before Ron Osborne pokes his political nose into it all. I'll have the address e-mailed to you within a few minutes."

O'Malley did not give a vocal dismissal, but his body language said it all. He was worried, irritated, and had nothing to say. Avery gathered up the papers he had slid to her and gave Ramirez a nod. They left together in a hurry. If there were any speculative eyes on them as they made their exit, she did not notice them. She was far too focused on having to tell the parents about their daughter's murder.

***

Terry and Julia Osborne lived in a gorgeous two-story house in the Back Bay area. The subdivision Avery and Ramirez drove down to reach their home was filled with lots reaching well into the million-dollar range. She knew that Terry Osborne had no political aspirations like his brother, but he *was* one of Boston's most coveted real estate agents. She was sure he got some of the most up-to-date scoops on available land through Ron Osborne, city councilman, but that was none of Avery's concern (nor did she really care) as she and Ramirez stepped up onto the Osbornes' porch.

She could hear a woman's wailing from within the house, apparently Julia Osborne in the midst of accepting news of her daughter's death. Still, the door was answered within twenty seconds. Terry Osborne was clearly in a state of shock. When he looked at Avery and Ramirez, he blinked his eyes rapidly, as if trying to adjust to some other part of the world that was not the misery currently within his home.

"Mr. Osborne," Avery said, "I'm Detective Black and this is my partner, Detective Ramirez. I know this is an impossible time for you, but we were hoping you could help us by answering some questions. We'd obviously like to catch the killer as quickly as we can."

"Yes, come on in," Osborne said. He turned away without much of an expression and walked deeper into his house like he was sleepwalking.

They followed him into the kitchen where he went to a very nice and elaborate wine rack. He selected a bottle of red and poured himself a very tall glass. Avery noted that it was a bottle of Houdini Napa Valley—a bottle Avery was pretty sure went for at least two hundred dollars. He sipped on it absently, almost like he had forgotten the two detectives were standing there.

"We'll make this as quick as possible," Avery said, still hearing the sniffling and wails coming from elsewhere in the house. "First of all, do you know why Sarah would have been out on that side of town?"

Terry shook his head. "She was working part time with a public outreach group…helping kids read and all that. I'm ashamed to say that I don't know where that took her. I guess it's possible she was there for work…I don't know."

"Do you know the name of the outreach program?" Avery asked.

"Helping Hands," he said. "I've got a card somewhere, I think…"

He started to walk out of the kitchen but Avery stopped him. "That's okay, Mr. Osborne. We can contact them."

She could tell that he was trying to keep busy. He was trying to occupy himself, to busy his mind with something else. But she also knew that when he ran out of things to do and questions to answer, he was going to crumble.

"Do you know if Sarah had any friends that might have been questionable? Anyone you weren't really a fan of her hanging out with?"

"No. I don't think so. I never really…well, I didn't know anything about her life, you know? I was always working and—"

She sensed him about to break and did her best to keep him afloat a while longer by offering another question.

"How about a boyfriend?" Avery asked.

Terry's face went blank, but they got an answer from a woman's voice from behind them. Julia Osborne had come into the kitchen. Her face was streaked with running mascara and she looked like a phantom. Her bottom lip was quivering and her hair was a mess.

"No boyfriends," she said. Her voice was raspy from having wept so much during the last hour and a half. "She ended a pretty serious relationship last year and has been single ever since. And in terms of friends…she didn't really have many. Just the kids she helped at Helping Hands. She was a sweet girl but…always kept to herself."

60

"Do you know the name of the ex?" Avery asked.

"Yeah. Denny Cox. But looking at him would be a waste of your time. He's a pretty good kid. Used to be a cop."

"Used to be?" Ramirez asked.

"Yes. He was fired not too long ago. After he and Sarah broke up."

Avery and Ramirez shared a look that they had come to use as almost another sort of language. With a simple nod of her head, Ramirez took his leave from the kitchen and headed back outside to call the station and ask for a check on Denny Cox.

"Is there anything else you can think of that I might need to know?" Avery asked.

Julia looked at the floor, as if embarrassed, and then nodded. "I was in her room just now…looking through her things…wanting something to hold just to sort of be with her—"

She started weeping here, her breath coming in huge hitching sobs. She held out her hand and offered something to Avery. Avery took it and saw that it was a plastic bag. There were six pills inside of it. Two had dollar signs on them and the other four had smiley faces.

Ecstasy, she thought. *And this is how her mother finds out. My God…*

"I don't want to know what it is," Julia said. "I want you to have it to see if it helps you find the man that did this."

Avery took it and said nothing. She looked back to the kitchen, where Terry was quickly downing the contents of his wine glass.

"Thank you for your cooperation," Avery said. "Please don't hesitate to call the station if you think of anything else that might be of use. Until then, please take care. Do you have anyone to come be with you?"

"My brother-in-law is on his way," Julia said. "He'll be damned sure we find who did this."

Avery nodded and gave her quick goodbyes to Terry and Julia. She did not want to be there when Ron Osborne showed up with a million questions and his inflated ego. She made her way back through the kitchen and the long hallway toward the front door. When she stepped out onto the porch, Ramirez was just getting off of the phone.

"Anything?" Avery asked.

"Oh yeah," he said. "Denny Cox, fired from the force ten months ago. And once I got the details, I actually remember hearing about it. He got caught with a prostitute in his patrol car. And he wasn't arresting her, if you get my drift."

"That's pretty lewd, but it doesn't really make him a suspect for—"

"Oh, it gets better," he said. "When Denny was fifteen, his father's shed caught on fire in their backyard. No reason...the fire department never found a source. This was the same year that there was a small fire started behind the dugouts on the baseball field at Desmond High School. Want to guess who was seen scampering away from the field when the teachers arrived?"

Avery wasted no time with guessing. She headed for the driver's side of the car and asked, "You got an address?"

CHAPTER THIRTEEN

When the address led them back into D3 territory—about six miles away from where the remains of Sarah Osborne had been ditched—it seemed like Denny Cox was indeed their man. It all seemed too circumstantial to not be a hot lead. Avery, though, always felt a degree of suspicion when something came together a little too easily. And this whole procurement of information on Denny Cox had basically fallen into her lap.

It was 6:37 when she parked in front of Denny's house. It was a basic little one-story house, a far cry from the Osborne residence they had just left. As they walked up to the porch, Avery saw a dead plant sitting next to the door on the front porch. The vinyl siding was starting to peel and grow mildew.

She rang the doorbell twice, having to push hard for it to work. Within seconds, a young man of about twenty-five or so answered the door. He was slightly overweight and had a scrubby few days' growth of beard.

He also appeared to be drunk. It was apparent in the way he wobbled on his feet, the blinking gaze to his eyes, and the unapologetic way in which he looked Avery up and down like a slab of meat.

"Hey there, Officers," he said. "Oops, no…Detectives, right?"

"That's right," Avery said. "Detectives Black and Ramirez. And you're Denny Cox, yes?"

"That's me," he said. "I was wondering how long it would take before you guys started questioning me. I figured I had until tomorrow at least. If I'd known you were coming so soon, I would have stopped at two beers. Maybe."

"And how did you know we were coming?" Avery asked.

"I saw the news about Sarah. It was on the local news at five o'clock."

Shit, Avery thought. *This could potentially get out of hand a lot faster than O'Malley thought.*

"You dated her for a while, right?" Ramirez asked.

"That I did," Cox said. His words were slurred and he seemed to be finding far too much amusement in the situation.

"And why did you break up?" Avery asked.

Cox looked at them for a moment with his drunken stare. It was clear to Avery that she and Ramirez were not going to be invited in—and it would be the second time in two days. When she thought of how things had gone with Adam Wentz, she heard a small alarm

63

sound in her head; she was going to have to keep an eye on Ramirez if Cox got out of hand.

Sadly, though, it was also clear to her that in his current state, Denny Cox was not going to be of much help.

"She was too young," Denny answered. "Only four years younger than me, but when I started working on the force she got all possessive. She was always griping that I didn't spend enough time with her. Plus, a cop dating a young girl...there's too much ribbing and jokes from the guys. It got old."

"And did you see her much after that?" Avery asked.

"Once. She got stoned off of her ass and called me up. I brought her over here and we had sex."

"You said she was stoned...do you know what she was on?"

"Coke, probably. She was sneaky about it, but she liked her cocaine." He snickered here and added: "But Mommy, Daddy, and Big Ol' Uncle Ron had no idea."

"You know for a fact she did drugs?" Avery asked.

"Yes. And she was damned good at hiding it. She drank here and there, too. But her big draws were cocaine and ecstasy."

"And as someone joining the force, you were okay with this?"

"It wasn't my business, you know? She and I had fun together...and during that last little while, I think it was mostly because of the drugs. So I let her have her fun. I was her boyfriend, not her father."

"Do you know who her dealer was?"

Cox chuckled and shook his head. "No. She kept that hush-hush—especially when I started talking about joining the force. But really, I think she was mostly concerned about her family finding out—especially her shithead political weasel of an uncle."

"Mr. Cox," Avery said, quickly trying to swerve the attention away from Cox's obvious disdain for the Osborne family, "what can you tell me about the two marks on your record that involve fire?"

"What marks? You mean that bullshit from high school about the dugouts? Yeah, that was dumb. A mistake I made to piss off the boyfriend of a girl I liked. Some stupid jock. I was fifteen. You think that makes me a candidate for murdering someone?"

It occurred to Avery that she had not seen the news reports. How much did the media know? If they weren't reporting anything about the way the people were being killed, she certainly didn't want to tip her hand to the likes of a man like Denny Cox. She figured if he *had* heard that little tidbit, he would have said something about it by now.

"No, it does not," Avery said. "But as a former cop, you know we have to speak to everyone connected to Sarah. You said it yourself…you knew it was just a matter of time before someone came to ask you some questions."

"There's also the matter of your father's shed burning down," Ramirez said. "And then the thing with the prostitute. You don't really have a very clean record."

Cox leaned against the doorframe and again looked Avery up and down. "You know…I know who you are, Detective Black. *Avery.* Most men were all pissy when you came on board in Boston. But I didn't see the big deal. Nice to look at…awesome record."

His eyes leered just a little too long. To get his attention, she moved her hand to her hip to reveal the Mace and the Glock holstered there.

"That's neither here nor there, Mr. Cox. We just wanted to ask you about—"

"Sarah, I know," he interrupted. "Yeah, I bet O'Malley and his boys are about to shit themselves over this. Niece of a councilman. I also saw where there's some disagreements over what district gets this high-profile case. I bet you two are working hard to get this one wrapped up, huh?"

"We are," Ramirez said, stepping forward. "So if you could please stop undressing my partner with your eyes and answer some fucking questions, that would be helpful."

"Settle down now," Cox said. "What the hell are you? A knight in shining armor or something?" He then leaned in and, in a hushed whisper, added: "You tapping that, my man?"

Ramirez moved too fast for Avery to stop him. He took one huge step forward and threw a right-handed punch at Cox.

Cox moved with surprising speed as well. He not only dodged the punch but caught Ramirez's arm and twisted it and pushed it hard against the doorframe. Ramirez instantly went for his sidearm but Avery stepped in to save a terrible situation from becoming even worse.

She shoved Ramirez back hard, causing Cox to release his arm. Cox then came at her, bringing his right hand back. Maybe it was because he was drunk, or maybe it was just because he was not taking the news of the death of an ex-girlfriend well, but he was apparently not taking the repercussions of his actions into account.

Avery attacked faster, though. She jabbed out a hard right hand, palm out and fingers curled. She struck him twice in rapid succession in the ribs. Cox dropped to his knee, gasping for breath. Ramirez stepped up again, going for his cuffs.

"No," Avery said, wheeling on him. She pushed him back a step and spoke as quietly as she could, not wanting Cox to overhear it and report the conversation at the station—where he would clearly be within an hour.

"What the—?" Ramirez began.

"That's twice in the past two days," she said. "You can't go after someone just because they speak to me in a degrading way or look at me a certain way. You're smarter than that. And quite frankly, it's pissing me off. While we're on the clock, I'm your partner…not your fucking babysitter."

Ramirez scowled at her but said nothing. In fact, he gave a quick nod of the head and went back to the car without a word. Avery took a deep calming breath and then turned back to Cox.

"That was pretty stupid," she said.

"Yeah," he grunted, now on his hands and knees.

"You know what comes next. You either get up and come calmly with me or I'm going to cuff you right here. I might just be mad enough to pull your shoulder back a little too hard. You know that cracking noise you sometimes hear when you bring a perp's arms behind their back a little too fast?"

Cox spit at her feet as he slowly started to get to his own. "I'd like to see you try it, bitch."

She smiled, clenched her fist, and showed him.

CHAPTER FOURTEEN

Avery had seen the A1 headquarters in disarray a few times. It usually happened when a new huge case broke or just as a promising lead came in and had everyone in a fervor to work together to wrap the case up. But when Avery and Ramirez arrived back at the station with Cox in tow, the place was a circus.

There were a few news vans in the parking lot as she parked. She led the way across the rear lot with Ramirez escorting Denny Cox. She heard a reporter say something loudly. Within seconds, four people were rushing across the back lot, one of whom was a cameraman. As she lowered her head and continued for the building, Avery also saw a few unfamiliar cop cars. She checked the tags and the decals and cursed under her breath.

Cops from the B3 district, she thought. *Great. Apparently they're going to ride this thing into the ground.*

Just as a reporter and a cameraman reached them, Avery was at the door, ushering Denny Cox inside.

"Excuse me," the reporter said. "Is this man under arrest for the killings and burnings?"

She said nothing, but Denny Cox sure as hell did.

"They came to my house and went nuts," he said, his drunken slur seeming to draw out each word. "Beat the shit out of me because they don't have any real leads."

Ramirez gave him a push and they were all through the doors and away from the reporters.

"What the hell is *that* about?" Ramirez asked Avery.

"There were B3 cars out there," she said. "I'm betting they went to the news, hoping the attention would throw us off."

As they ventured further into the station, the circus continued. She saw a few men in B3 uniforms, including the one who had confronted them earlier in the day at the latest site. He was arguing with Officer Finley. Connelly was in the fray, too, doing everything he could to appear calm. When Connelly saw Avery, he waved her over urgently.

"You got this handled?" Avery asked Ramirez, gesturing to Cox.

"Yeah. See if you can sort all of this out."

Avery quickly made her way over to where Connelly was in the midst of a heated debate between Finley and one of the B3 officers. The tag on his uniform read Simmons.

"What the hell is going on here?" Avery asked.

"Too much at once," Connelly said. "Someone over at B3 leaked the story to the press. In the last hour, the media has been reporting that there's an interdepartmental rivalry going on."

"That's not exactly accurate," Simmons said. "Although, we..."

Simmons trailed off here, looking behind Avery. She turned and followed his gaze. He was looking at Ramirez ushering Cox to an interrogation room.

"What the fuck?" Simmons said, not quite in a yell but nowhere near quiet. "Is that Denny Cox?"

"Yes, it is," Avery said. "Do you know him?"

He looked at her with such venom that she thought he might throw a punch or shove her. "He used to be a B3 cop."

Connelly's eyes grew wide. "Are you shitting me? This is unbelievable."

"I don't care what department he was with," Avery said. "He was fired for very good reasons and also has a history of arson. Add to that the fact that he was an ex-boyfriend of Sarah Osborne, the latest victim, and there's more than enough reason to bring him in."

"Jesus," Simmons said.

"Seems like karma if you ask me," Finley said. "You tattle to the media on us and now there are cameras rolling everywhere when one of your boys gets arrested."

"Everyone calm down," Connelly said. "Finley...I need you to go ahead and release Adam Wentz. After that, I don't care what you do, just stay away from these B3 pricks."

"Hey, watch your mouth," Simmons said.

"You're in my station, asshole. I don't need to watch my mouth." Ignoring him, Connelly then turned to Avery. "I need a word with you in private. Come on."

He led her through the cramped station and to his office. He shut the door behind them and rubbed at his temples.

"This is a mess," he said. "This is just one huge clusterfuck, Avery. Now please...tell me there is a really good reason for having that ex-B3 cop here in cuffs."

"Aside from his record, he also got violent when we questioned him."

"In your opinion, is he our guy?"

"It's too soon to tell, sir."

"Cut that nonsense. What's your gut telling you?"

She thought about it for a moment and then shook her head. "Probably not. If he was the killer and has been dumping bodies at the rate we're finding them burned, I doubt he'd have been drinking heavily—and Denny Cox is pretty drunk at the moment. If he was the killer, he'd want to stay alert and ready just in case we caught on to him."

"But is there a chance he's our guy?" Connelly asked.

"There's always a chance, sir."

"Well, if we can't nail him for it within an hour, I'm letting him go. This just makes an already screwed-up situation even worse."

"Understood."

"Now," he said, "as if things aren't bad enough, I need you to head to O'Malley's office. The fucking FBI showed up two hours ago and are pushing against us. I need you to talk to him and see if you can work your magic. And I need you on it *now*."

She left Connelly's office as he started rubbing at his temples in frustration again. She hurried down the hallway to O'Malley's larger office. She knocked on the door, which was already cracked, and entered following O'Malley's loud *"Come in."*

She entered the office and saw that O'Malley looked just as flustered as Connelly. The FBI agent that was standing at the edge of O'Malley's desk and rifling through documents, however, looked unreasonably calm.

"Special Agent Duggan, this is Detective Avery Black," O'Malley said. "She's our very best. She's also the lead on this case."

Duggan extended his hand and gave hers a hearty shake. He looked to be in his late forties. He was well-polished right down to his beard. "Nice to meet you," Duggan said. "I hear you're the very best in the A1."

"Let's hope so," she said. "What can I do for you?"

"Well, I'm not here to run the show. I just wanted to sort of partner up with the best there is. This guy you just brought in…do you think he's the culprit?"

"Honestly, no."

Duggan smiled and then looked to O'Malley. "I don't either," he said. "Your chief and I had a little bet. Seems he won…he was pretty sure you'd not think this is our guy either. Now, what makes you think he's not the guy?"

"He'd be 'fessing up by now," Avery said. "He'd want to claim the crimes. He'd also not be one beer away from being absolutely hammered if he was in the middle of some weird killing and burning spree. He's also pretty drunk…and someone in the midst of a killing spree would want a clear head at all times."

"You've got a smart girl here," Duggan said.

O'Malley nodded, but it looked like it pained him to admit it. "Yeah, I know. But I can't just let this guy go. The pieces are all too coincidental. Even if *we* know it, the media doesn't. There's too much pressure."

"So you're keeping him here?" Avery asked. "You might want to talk to Connelly. He wants him out of here in an hour if nothing solid comes up."

"Black, I have no choice for now. Look...help Agent Duggan however you can. But for now, I'm working under the premise that we've got our guy. So you can give it a rest for now."

"Chief O'Malley," Duggan said, "you have two very qualified people saying this is not your man and—"

"With all due respect, you come talk to me when you have a bloodthirsty media and a paranoid public to think about. Until then...thanks for your help, Agent Duggan...but you can take your leave now. You, too, Black."

Avery shook her head and chuckled. "No big deal," she said when Duggan was gone. "You're wrong. And that means I'll see you within another day or so, wondering if you'll actually admit to being wrong."

"Get out of here, Black," O'Malley spat.

Avery did as he requested, barely aware that Agent Duggan was following after her. It was like being shadowed by a wraith or some sort of demon. Sure, she knew he only wanted to help, but it was like some weight pulling at her as the pressure of her superiors and the media tightened in around her.

With Duggan trailing her, she knew that she needed time away from the frenzy of the A1. Just a small break where she could get out some frustration. With Duggan still following behind her as she made her way to her office, she turned to the agent and tried to be as friendly as possible.

"I'm stepping out for an hour or so," she said. "Has O'Malley given you my contact information?"

"He has."

"Then call me if you need me."

"If I might ask...where are you headed that might be more important than what's happening right now?"

In a cold and almost calculated voice, she answered: "I'll be back soon. For right now, I just need to hit something."

CHAPTER FIFTEEN

He wasn't sure why the sight of ash made him feel so at peace. It was something he had struggled with since his childhood. By looking at a pile of ash, he felt not only powerful, but simple and peaceful. It was the same with dust. In the same way that a piece of wood could be burned to nothing more than a weightless pile of ash, bricks and concrete could also be broken down to their basest form—useless dust.

This was especially true of the human body. The human body was a marvelous thing, from the smooth skin to the unidentifiable cells within it. But when it was met with intense fire, the human body was no better than a common piece of wood. It was reduced to mere ash, a pile of almost nothing that could be placed into a bag and thrown away without a second thought.

A bag…or an urn.

He sat in his rollaway chair and turned to face the shelf that sat to the far side of the room. The shelf, much like the room, was immaculately cleaned. It was empty except for a small desk, his chair, the shelf with the urns, and three buckets of a homemade chemical mixture that were pushed far into the corner. The floor was concrete and the walls were made of cinderblock. A group of glass urns sat on the shelf. There were eight in all—but there had once been ten. He'd taken the other two with him the last time he had carried the bodies out and dumped them. He had almost decided to keep them but had come to the conclusion that the urns should stay with the remains. It seemed more pure that way.

Slowly, he got up and walked to the back of the room. The place was slit only by a single overhead bulb. There were no windows and even if there were, no light would get in. He was currently about fifteen feet underground, sitting directly below the house he had been raised in. It should have been relatively cold in the room but over the last few days, it had gotten rather warm.

And there was a foul smell, too.

The smell came from the back of the room, from the very place he was now walking toward. Along the back of the wall, there was a large metal door. It looked very much like the door of a meat locker but was reinforced by a thick board that slid through a metal clasp, holding the already-secure locking mechanism in place.

He slid the board out and placed it against the wall. He then opened the door by its U-shaped pressurized handle. He opened it now and looked inside. When he did, the foul smell increased tenfold.

He was used to it, though. It didn't bother him in the slightest as he peered inside.

The room was three feet deep and five feet wide. While it was contained in the cinderblock of the cellar he did his work in, he had spent the better part of a year insulating it. The walls were made of sheets of steel and stone. The stone wall was about a foot thick, with a layer of steel on both sides.

There were char marks here and there along the walls but he was pleased with how his handiwork had held up. The ceiling had buckled a bit but would hold up for at least another three or four fires.

So far, he had burned two bodies inside of it. He'd done his very best to clean up after each one but there was still a lingering dust of ash on the floor. There was no vent of any kind within the room, so the room still contained a great deal of the heat from the two fires and the test fires that had come before them.

And soon—perhaps as early as tomorrow—there would be even more heat inside. The box contained fire much better than he had ever hoped. And over the years, he had learned not only how to properly set fires, but how to make them stronger and how to control them. It was something of an art, an art that he was still learning to perfect.

He smiled into the room and slowly closed the door again. After he slid the board back through the metal loop, he walked over to the shelf. He took one of the urns down and plucked it lightly. It made a pleasant *ting* that rang musically through the room.

He opened it and looked at the emptiness inside.

He smiled again, knowing that it would not be empty for very long.

CHAPTER SIXTEEN

Avery never even thought about going back home. If she'd retreated home with her tail between her legs after being dismissed by O'Malley (especially in front of an FBI agent) she would have felt like jumping out of her own skin. Instead, she had headed straight for the gym. She took Krav Maga classes twice a week and although this was not the night of either of her classes, she knew that there were always people hanging around the mats, looking to spar.

When you were an attractive woman not yet in her forties, finding a random sparring partner was easy.

Of course, the cocky look on the face of the man who had volunteered to spar with her became one of confusion, then embarrassment, and then fear. He had gone through that whole range of emotion in less than a minute.

Currently, she was maneuvering herself around his back with his right arm trapped. As she locked in the arm bar, she felt her mind drift off, almost letting her muscles and joints go into some sort of autopilot. She thought of what was going on at headquarters and how FBI interference—not to mention media attention—could make this case harder. She also thought about how irresponsible Ramirez had been on two occasions, one right behind the other. It was not like him. While he could be a hothead from time to time, she was still pretty sure the two altercations had come from a protective feeling he now had for her because they had finally shared a bed.

She felt the man trying to buckle under her, trying to roll her to the left. He was strong but not nearly as fast or as intuitive as Avery. She moved her right leg, wrapped it around his back, and then quickly brought her arms up to his chest. She caught him mid-roll, stopped his momentum, and was able to not only pin him to the mat in a rear naked choke, but she also managed to trap his right leg beneath him. He wasn't going anywhere. Now, all Avery had to do was gently apply pressure. She did this gradually, feeling his body tense up beneath her as her train of thought reconnected.

She thought of her meeting with Sloane and how she had learned the basics of how an arsonist's mind worked. It seemed eerily simple and she could not figure out why she was having such a hard time grasping it. As of late, it seemed that she was having a hard time understanding *anyone*: the killer, Ramirez, even her own daughter.

73

Thinking of Rose, she wondered where she was right now. She wondered if Rose had finally blown off her anger and unblocked her own mother from Facebook. She wondered if—

Her thoughts were again broken, this time by the sound of the man beneath her tapping rapidly at the mat in submission.

She released him and he rolled away, getting to his feet slowly. He looked back at her with an embarrassed smile as Avery sat calmly on the mat, catching her breath. She had worked up a nice sweat and she was starting to feel at peace again.

"I'd say it doesn't sting to be beaten since it was by a beautiful woman," her random sparring partner said. "But that would be a lie. Losing sucks regardless."

"It does," she said.

And before allowing the time to let the conversation get awkward, she left the mat and headed into the gym. She spent some time at the punching bags, enjoying the almost percussive sound they made against her fists when she worked up her rhythm and speed. She then worked on her lower-body attack. She didn't stop until her muscles were sore and sweat was stinging her eyes.

She made her way to the shower, feeling that she had worked some of the day's frustrations off. She considered calling Ramirez, knowing of at least one other physical activity that did wonders for working off stress. But given the day they'd had, she would only be using him and he didn't deserve that.

She left the gym and headed out onto the street. It was just after seven and the clogged traffic of people getting off work had thinned out. She had a brisk ten-block walk ahead of her, something she enjoyed from time to time. It was an especially good little exercise following a workout at the gym.

But four minutes into her walk, all thoughts of exercise and stress release were forgotten.

Just up ahead of her on the other side of the street, she caught sight of Rose.

***

She was walking into a small café that Avery had passed countless times but had never visited. There was a young man with her. They were holding hands and Rose was laughing about something as they stepped inside. Avery stopped for a moment, feeling her common sense and her motherly instincts at war. In the end, it wasn't much of a match; she crossed the street and headed for the diner.

She peered in through the glass but couldn't see them. The place didn't appear to be too busy but Avery couldn't get a clear view from the street. With a sigh, she pushed at the door and went inside. The place smelled of coffee and freshly baked pastries. From what she could tell, the place catered to a younger crowd, making Avery feel a little out of her element—especially after having just come from the gym and dressed in a baggy hoodie and workout pants.

She spotted Rose and her apparent beau near the back of the café. A waitress was speaking to them, jotting down their orders. Avery walked slowly in that direction and moved in just as the waitress walked away. As luck would have it, there was a third chair at their table, positioned alone on the side opposite them. Avery walked over as if she had been invited but was not so bold as to take a seat.

Rose looked up, confused at first, but then falling into a state of absolute terror. The guy looked equally confused. Avery checked him over quickly and found that he was exactly the type of guy she imagined Rose would go after: tall, dark hair, scruff from his ears down, and one of those stupid ear-stretchers in each of his ear lobes.

"Hi, Rose," Avery said.

"What are you doing here?" Rose asked.

"I saw you come in and thought I'd stop by and say hello."

"You saw me come in?" Rose asked, clearly not believing her. "Since when do you frequent coffee shops?"

"I don't," Avery said. "I was leaving the gym on the other end of the block and saw you coming in." She then looked to the young man and gave a small and rather insincere wave. "Hi. I'm Avery—Rose's mother."

"Oh. Nice to meet you," he said, uncertain.

"Mom, are you really doing this right here, right now?" Rose asked.

"Hey," the guy said. "It's okay, Rose." He gave Avery a smile and reached across the table to shake Avery's hand. "I'm Marcus," he said.

She shook the offered hand but wasn't fooled by the gesture. His expression alone spoke of arrogance. He didn't think there was any way an unexpected visit from an estranged mother was going to throw him off of his game.

"Hi, Marcus," Avery said. "Pleased to meet you."

"Marcus is my boyfriend," Rose said.

"I assumed as much," Avery said with a smile.

"Now that you've met him, can you leave?" Rose asked.

75

"Not yet," Avery said. "How are you doing, Rose?"

"I'm fine, with the exception of my mother embarrassing the hell out of me and trying to act like everything is fine after she blew me off for the hundredth time yesterday."

"Rose, look…I'm sorry. You know I can't just blow off work when huge cases pop up. It's part of my job."

"Well, then get back to your job and leave us alone."

Avery knew she deserved it but at the same time, enough was enough.

"Marcus, how long have you and my daughter been dating?" Avery asked.

"Mom!" Rose objected.

Marcus tried to seem unfazed. He shrugged and said, "About a month or so, I guess."

"Ah, you'd think my own daughter would tell me something like that, now wouldn't you?"

"I don't know," Marcus said. "She's told me about you guys. She's told me about your job. It kind of sucks."

"My job, you mean?" she asked.

"No…that you're always blowing her off."

"Marcus—" Rose said.

Avery looked back and forth between them. On the one hand, this little creep had no right to speak to her like that but on the other hand, she had come in here unannounced and had taken them both by surprise.

"Are you trying to sweep in and be the understanding hero while her mother busts her ass on the streets?" Avery asked. "Is that it?"

"No, that's not it at all," Marcus said. The arrogance was back in his face. He seemed to think that just because her daughter had eyes for him, he was untouchable. "But let me tell you…if that *was* my intent, you would make it pretty easy on me."

Avery smirked at him. She started to clench and unclench her fists, trying to make sure she didn't cause a scene. She looked at Rose and said, "You've got a real winner on your hands here."

"Shut up, Mom. God…I can't believe you'd do this!"

"Marcus, what do you do for a living?" Avery asked.

"Mom—"

Marcus chuckled and got up from the table. "I'm not getting the third degree," he said, burning a stare into Avery. He then turned to Rose and said, "Call me when Mommy says it's okay."

He then leaned down and kissed her. He did it in a teasing way, just to get under Avery's skin. Their open mouths left little to the

76

imagination; there was more than a little tongue at play. Marcus broke the kiss, didn't even bother looking back at either of them, and walked for the door.

"Proud of yourself?" Rose asked.

"Rose...I only came in because you aren't returning my calls and you've blocked me on social media."

"And? What do you expect? Mom...you fell through *again.* I'm tired of it. And crashing a date isn't any way to make up for it. Do you have *any* idea how embarrassing that was?"

"Well, I didn't come in here to grill your boyfriend, believe me. But he got high and mighty, so I retaliated."

"But Marcus is none of your business," Rose said. She was speaking loudly now, attracting the attention of some of the other patrons. "And you know what...for a detective, you can be pretty stupid, you know that? What do you think this little intervention is going to do? What do you think is going to happen after this? I'm going to call him and whine about my obsessive bitch of a mother and he's going to come over to comfort me. Want to guess how that'll end?"

"Rose, don't talk to me like that," Avery said. It stung...not just the imagery it brought up but the fact that her daughter would speak to her in such a way so easily.

"It's okay, Mom," she said. "We've already slept together."

"Rose—"

"I've been on the pill for about three months now. That's something you might know if you gave a damn enough to actually hang out and talk to me."

"Rose, can't we just—"

"No!"

This time she *did* shout. The café went quiet as a flush of heat raced through Avery. All eyes were on them now and in that moment, she felt weaker than she had in a very long time.

"Don't call me anymore," Rose said, getting up from the table, her voice still loud and thunderous. "Just forget about me. You do it *so* well. That and ruining everything!"

With that, Rose took her leave, storming toward the door. Slowly, conversation returned to the other tables. Avery stood there, staring down at the tabletop, wondering just where in the hell things had started to turn so wrong for her and Rose. For a moment there a few days ago, it seemed like things were getting better. So what had happened?

You chose work over her, stupid, she told herself.

A waitress approached from seemingly out of nowhere. She looked very uncomfortable to be next to her but did her duty anyway. "Can I get you anything, ma'am?"

"I don't guess you serve tequila, huh?" she asked.

The waitress frowned and walked off without another word.

Several moments later, Avery did the same. She stepped back out into the cool night and headed home, hoping to find some answers and solace there. She silenced her phone, sure that Connelly or Agent Duggan would call, and walked to her apartment, trying to remember a time when she had ever felt more alone.

CHAPTER SEVENTEEN

It was ridiculous, Avery thought, that an eighteen-year-old could make her feel so defeated, alone, and embarrassed. It was one of the least glamorous parts of being the mother of a teenager on the verge of going into the real world. Worse, though, was that she felt like she was totally failing at being a mother.

What truly bothered Avery was that when she got home from the café, she wanted to bury that sense of failure in her work. Her work, after all, was what had caused her relationship with Rose to suffer. Frustrated, she took the files out of her laptop bag and practically threw them on the coffee table.

She sighed as she went to the refrigerator. She took a moment to decide between wine and beer and ended up sitting down at the table with a very tall glass of moscato. She had just enough time to read the first few lines of the coroner's report from the first set of remains before the vibrating buzz of her cell phone interrupted her.

She'd silenced it for a reason, but when she saw that it was Ramirez, she picked it up. Before answering it, though, she felt a little uneasy. She had no idea what sort of direction a conversation with him might take right now, but she also knew that she had never been so totally aware of how alone she was until after coming home from the latest failed conversation with Rose.

"Hey," she said almost flippantly.

"Hey, Avery."

A long pause followed this—a pause that irritated her because it made her feel as if whatever chemistry they had between them had devolved into some sort of basic middle school fling. The sort of fling where everything was always awkward and there was never anything of substance to talk about. Ramirez must have sensed this, too; out of nowhere, he decided to get right to the point—which was very unlike him.

"So what's going on?" he asked. "Are we okay?"

"We're fine," she said.

"The other night didn't change things?"

"Of course it changed things," she said. "But that has nothing to do with the past two days. This case is dragging me down and there's all this tension and drama with Rose going on behind the scenes."

"I get it," he said. "Is there anything I can do? Do you need me to come over?"

She wasn't sure why this comment made her slightly angry, but it did. And before she was able to understand this, she was letting that anger shape her words as she spoke them.

"No, I don't," she said. "You should know by now that I'm not one of these women that needs a man to feel safe and secure. I'm with you most of the day at work, which means there's really nothing you can do about the case weighing on me. And no offense, but I'm not even about to bring you into things with Rose. So thanks, but no thanks."

He was quiet on the other end for a moment. When he spoke, his words were soft and deliberate. "I'm going to be honest here," he said. "Avery, I think the world of you and if I had my way, I'd be over there right now. And that's why I'm going to call it a day. I know you've got a lot on your plate right now but it's no need to be a bitch to me."

"A bitch?" Avery asked. "What have I done to be a bitch? Not let you come over and kiss me and stroke my hair and tell me everything is okay? How's that being a bitch?"

She barely heard his sigh from the other end but it *was* there. "Bye, Avery. I'll see you at work tomorrow."

Before she could say anything else, Ramirez killed the call. She rolled her eyes and slammed her phone down on top of the folder. Before she could let her anger rise up any further, she concentrated on the folder, focusing in once again on the coroner's report. She looked over the details of the scant remains of Keisha Lawrence, looking for something that might have been overlooked. She did the same for the still-growing file on Sarah Osborne and really did nothing more than commit it all to memory.

As she expected, though, there was nothing. The coroner and the guys at Forensics had looked at this thing from every angle. They had done exhaustive work and Avery knew she'd find nothing new.

Somehow, by the time she had looked through the reports, she had emptied her wine glass. She refilled it and attacked it right away. She knew that drinking was not the best form of therapy but at the moment it seemed to at least be making her care a little less about her problems with Rose and Ramirez.

She half-heartedly looked through the files as her second glass of wine got lower and lower. When that glass was empty, she refilled it, emptying the bottle. She then stood in the kitchen, staring at the fridge for a moment. She sipped slowly from the glass, feeling herself lean somewhere further away from tipsy and closer to drunk. She prided herself on knowing when to stop and had only gotten drunk on one occasion—and that had been while in college.

But maybe tonight would be the second time.

She stared at the fridge and her heart started to go cold. In the back of her head, a memory that she had pushed very far back started to bully its way forward.

Broken beer bottles from an opened fridge, a pool of amber liquid on the floor, mom screaming, Beth crying in the living room.

The memory was such a behemoth in her mind that she literally froze for a moment, unmoving and unblinking. She could even recall that the refrigerator door had been opened for so long that the interior light had shut itself off. She was pretty sure she had closed it and afterward, once her mother had stopped screaming and Beth had gone to bed, Avery had cleaned the spilled beer up.

Avery shuddered at the memory. Then, pushed more by the amount of wine she had drunk rather than by need or courage, she picked up her cell phone. She scrolled to "Beth" and pressed call.

She put the phone to her ear and listened to the ringing of her sister's phone for the first time in nineteen months.

It was answered on the third ring. "Hello?"

Beth's voice nearly made her weep. *God, I've missed her,* Avery thought.

"Hey," she said. "It's Avery."

"Oh." It was a genuine sound of surprise and the silence that followed was completely different than the silence she'd experienced with Ramirez forty minutes ago. This silence carried a sorrowful weight between the two phones.

"Am I bothering you?" Avery asked.

"No, not really. I'm just shocked to hear from you."

The southern twang in Beth's voice made Avery smile. Beth had been born and raised in West Virginia before Avery's parents had adopted her at the age of seven. And although they had moved to Maine and then Massachusetts through their childhood, that southern accent had never faded away.

"Well, my mind has been to some strange places today," Avery admitted. "I had this memory…this thought, I guess. It made me think about you. I sort of just wanted to check in. I know it seems like I've forgotten about you a lot of the time and…"

She didn't finish the statement. She purposefully stopped, hoping Beth would pick up the thread.

"Avery, that's okay," she said. "I could have called, too. But I chose not to. I figured you thought the same way. Mom and Dad died, you went off to college, I did my own thing. We separated. We moved on. It happens sometimes."

"But sisters," Avery said. "Sisters should be different."

"Do you still feel like my sister?" Beth asked.

"Of course I do. If I didn't, I sure as hell wouldn't have called you." She almost followed Beth's question up with the same question. She decided not to, though. She was actually afraid of what the answer might be. Beth had said time and time again how as an adopted kid, she never felt connected to Avery. She'd said these things when she was pissed or moody all through their teen years, though. As such, Avery had never thought much of it.

But now with years and physical distance between them, those old comments carried a sting with them.

"So what are you up to?" Beth asked. "Still with the Boston police?"

"Yes," Avery said, surprised by the attempt at conversation. "How about you? Are you still working for that...what was it? An ad firm?"

"It was, yeah. But I'm doing freelance design now."

"How's that going?" Avery asked.

"Pretty good." She paused, let out a sigh, and then added: "Look, Avery. Are we for real going to try to do this? Are we really going to pretend that it hasn't been a year and a half since we last spoke? Are we going to pretend that there isn't this...this *ghost* sitting between us every time we speak?"

"Beth, it's not a—"

"Let's be honest," Beth interrupted. "When we split apart, we went our separate ways. And we're not doing too bad for ourselves. Can't we just leave it at that? Maybe we're better when we're far apart—when we're just memories for each other."

"Is that what you'd prefer?" Avery asked.

"Yeah, it sort of is. Thinking about you and Mom and Dad and everything that happened...all it does is hurt. And I chose a while ago to not do that to myself."

"If that's what you want," Avery said.

"Thanks for calling, sis. But I'm going to go now."

Avery said nothing. Her apartment was so quiet that she heard the *click* when Beth ended the call.

She set her phone down softly on the kitchen table and slowly walked into the living room. She sat down on the couch and looked at the scattered files on the current case. She gave them only a cursory glance at first; her mind was elsewhere.

82

Let's do the math, she thought. *That's a daughter, a maybe-boyfriend, and an estranged sister that I have managed to drive further away in less than four hours. That's got to be some kind of a record. What the actual fuck is wrong with me?*

She was tempted to go to the fridge and start on the beer. But she knew that would only make things worse. It would make her more prone to overthinking her troubles *and* it would hinder her with a hangover in the morning.

Instead, she buried herself elsewhere…in the only other avenue she had ever really known to effectively absorb grief.

She turned back to her work, now more obsessed than ever with the case and finding a way to capture what was turning out to be a truly sadistic killer.

Quickly, her mind took a sharp and dark turn. There was somewhere else she had always turned when things had gotten hard. Had she not been three very tall glasses of wine into the night, she might have realized that this was something of a crutch for her. But she was pleasantly buzzed and her thoughts, while frantic, were also very easy to twist into shapes that made sense to her in that moment.

She found herself thinking of Howard Randall.

CHAPTER EIGHTEEN

With the same nervous sort of queasiness overcoming her that she always experienced when visiting Howard, Avery found herself being led through South Bay House of Corrections, nearing B-Level. The guards that led her were making it quite clear that they did not enjoy this detail, doing so without saying a single word.

With only their footfalls to break the silence, the guards led Avery to the same small conference room she'd visited a few times before. And just like on those previous visits, Howard Randall was seated at a rectangular table, sitting in a prim and proper manner. He smiled at her as she stepped into the room. The guards shut the doors behind her, leaving Avery alone with Howard.

"Avery, I can't even begin to explain how lovely it is to see you again."

Avery only nodded as she took her seat. Howard looked to be in pretty bad shape. He looked thinner than the last time she had seen him. Something about his face looked hollow and almost empty. Still, it pained her to admit that something about him made her feel almost at ease. He might be psychotic and selfish, but he was *familiar*.

And given the way she had handled her life as of late, she could use a little familiarity.

"Thanks for agreeing to meet with me," Avery said.

"Of course. I assume it's about this deplorable man that is burning his victims?"

"How did you—?"

She had nearly asked *how did you know?* but they had been through this same song and dance before. He had avenues to information within the prison walls. Avery wasn't sure where he got his information from but he had proven time and time again that he had very little problem keeping in the loop. This was especially true when it came to cases she was handling.

"It is," Avery admitted.

"You know, it almost hurts my feelings that you never visit just to see me or to chat," Howard teased, giving her a thin little smile.

"I'm sure you understand that I don't have much free time to just swing by and chat." What she thought but didn't say was: *If I can't make quality time for my own daughter, I'm certainly not going to make it for you.*

"Yes, I do understand," Howard said, a little arrogantly. "Well then, let's cut to the chase, shall we? What is it you need from me?"

"The mentality of someone that's so closely linked to arson…it's something I can't quite nail down."

"Arson?" Howard said, a little confused. "Why are you assuming arson has something to do with it? The man is burning bodies, not buildings."

"Because he's using fire almost like a weapon. He's using it almost as a symbol."

"Exactly," Howard said. "And if he's using fire for some sort of symbolic means, that does not necessarily mean he's an arsonist."

"But fire seems to be the most important aspect to this case. That or he has some sort of weird fixation on bones and ash. But you need fire to get to those things."

"Indeed. I agree one hundred percent. But still…the inclusion of fire in his murdering does not necessarily mean you're looking for an arsonist. That's like saying a killer that would kidnap people and drown them in a tub must surely be some sort of failed scuba diver." He chuckled at his own analogy; it was a dry and wretched sound.

Avery had considered this before but had not dwelled on it. The issue of fire seemed too important to *not* be the driving force behind the murders. But what if the killer was indeed only using it as a means to an end…a way to show off or eliminate evidence?

"Really, Avery," Howard said, crossing his arms. "I thought you were much smarter than this. I feel like you might be relying on me a little too much. Are you getting lazy?"

"No," she said, nearly offended by the accusation. "It's just rare to have such a relationship with someone who knows the minds of killers so well. As odd as it may be, you're one of the most reliable resources I have."

"I don't know if I should take that as an insult or a compliment," Howard said. "Either way, I suppose that makes us kindred spirits in an odd way, doesn't it?"

The thought of it made her want to shudder. But she'd be damned if she'd look weak in front of him.

"So what do you want me to do?" he asked. "Would you like me to drop you several hints? Are you hoping I might have some insight that will present you with a lead that you can claim as your own, solve the case and save the day?"

She wasn't sure how to respond. He had never been so confrontational. In fact, whenever she visited, he seemed to get an almost intellectual satisfaction from their conversations—from her cases. Perhaps that was no longer the case.

"No," she said. "I thought you might be able to lend some thoughts that might speed things along. That's all."

"Perhaps I could," he said. "But really, where is the fun in that? This killer…he seems to take pride in his work. More than that, he's *brave*. It's rather admirable really. You know, maybe I don't *want* to take your side every time, Avery. Maybe it would do you good to get out there and do the hard work yourself."

A simple response came to her lips, but she bit it back. *Fuck you.*

Instead, she replied: "So you'd be fine just letting this psycho continue to kidnap and burn these people? He's probably burning them alive, you know."

"Oh, I almost guarantee it," Howard said. "And maybe *that's* the important thing you should have been chasing this whole time rather than wasting your time studying arson. Now…I appreciate the visit, but I'm going to have to ask you to head along on your way."

"Are you—"

"Guard!" he shouted, interrupting her. "I'm done here."

Right away, one of the guards who had escorted her came into the room. He still had the same unpleasant look on his face as he approached Howard.

"Best of luck, Detective," Howard said.

Avery sat there, stunned for a moment. Howard Randall had *always* been full of surprises. But she had never expected this. Maybe he had just gotten tired of playing along with her cases when she had hit bottom.

Daughter, boyfriend, sister…now a killer to add to the list, she thought. *No one wants to be around me…not even Howard Randall.*

She slowly got up and headed for the exit. As she did, she thought about the almost riddle-like clue he'd dropped near the end.

…maybe that's the important thing you should have been chasing this whole time…

If the killer was burning his victims alive, that spoke of a whole new level to the case. It meant they were dealing with a man that was likely somewhere far beyond sadistic. It was one thing for someone to want to watch the world burn and quite another for someone to find a purpose and maybe even joy in the pain of the burning.

Maybe there are still some clues to be found on the bodies themselves, she thought. *At least what's left of them.*

With that thought in her head, she made her way back out of the prison thinking about teeth.

CHAPTER NINETEEN

She arrived back at the A1 half an hour later. She headed directly down to the lower levels, where Forensics took up most of the floor space. There were in-jokes about how all of the scientists and lab rats had been pushed down into the basement, but, truth be told, Avery enjoyed visiting this quieter and often calmer part of the building.

She headed for the office of Sandy Ableton, one of A1's two dental forensics experts. She didn't have to knock; Sandy's door was open and the unexpected sounds of Tom Petty's "Into the Great Wide Open" came spilling out. Avery poked her head in and knocked on the doorframe. Sandy looked up with a smile and motioned her inside.

"Avery, how are you?" she asked.

"Well, I was hoping you might have some sort of useful information from the dental findings in these burning deaths."

"Nothing new, I'm afraid," Sandy said. "We're still running a few tests on Sarah Osborne's molars, but that's likely not going to provide much to go on. And we've mined everything we can out of Keisha Lawrence's remains."

"Well, I was curious," Avery said. "Is there any way you can determine if the victim was killed before they were burned?"

Sandy raised an eyebrow, as if it was something she had not considered yet. "You feel like they might be burned alive?" she asked.

"I think it's a possibility we can't afford not to explore."

"Well, in some cases we could make an educated guess based solely on the condition of the gums and surrounding tissue. But in the case of Keisha Lawrence, the teeth had been totally stripped and burned of the gums. And while there was *some* remaining on Sarah Osborne's, it's not going to be enough to get you that sort of information."

"Okay," Avery said, quickly cycling through her new ideas. "Is there any way to determine how hot the teeth became while the body was burned?"

"I can give you a pretty good estimate, but nothing spot on. And you'd probably get the same lackluster answer off of the bone samples, too."

"An educated guess is all I'm looking for."

With that, Sandy typed in a few commands on the laptop that was sitting on her desk. "Into the Great Wide Open" had ended, giving way to "Mary Jane's Last Dance."

"Teeth, as you know," Sandy said, "are among the strongest bones in the human body. When exposed to extreme heat, they'll weaken but rarely will they start to decompose. We can gauge the approximate intensity of heat based on the amount they are weakened…just like any other bones, really."

She tapped a few more keys and then turned the laptop toward Avery so she could see it. She pointed to a section of a file and said, "Right there. Right around one thousand to eleven hundred degrees Fahrenheit."

"And what does a temperature that high tell you about the killer?" Avery asked.

"Well, it indicates that he knows what he's doing. Another four to eight hundred degrees and we're talking about cremation practices. Crematoriums usually burn bodies at somewhere between fourteen hundred and eighteen hundred degrees."

"So the fires this guy is setting aren't just random fires by some random firebug in other words."

Sandy shrugged. "I don't know for sure. That's above my pay grade. But yeah…to get to temperatures like that, it's more than just using some lighter fluid and striking a match."

"And do you know how crematoriums deal with teeth since they don't burn down?"

"Yes, they're usually ground up just like bones. I'm not sure what sort of a machine does it, but with human remains that are cremated, it's very rare to find anything other than ash."

Avery nodded, taking it all in. She had started to think that their man might have had some sort of connection with a crematorium but based on what Sandy was telling her, this man wasn't *quite* that efficient. So that had to leave other links that they had not discovered yet. Crematoriums might certainly be worth looking into, but Avery wasn't so sure it was the most pertinent place to start looking.

"Can I help with anything else?" Sandy asked.

Avery tried to think if there were any other questions that needed to be asked but was interrupted by the ringing of her cell phone. She grabbed it and saw that it was Connelly. A slow sinking feeling started in her stomach.

"This is Avery," she said.

"Black, where are you?"

"With Forensics. What's up?"

"I need you out here ASAP. We've got another body."

CHAPTER TWENTY

Having seen the state of the two previous victims as little more than ash and bones, Avery was not mentally ready for what she saw at the third crime scene. She could tell right away that something was different about this scene when she parked her car behind O'Malley's. The location was very similar to the first scene where the remains of Keisha Lawrence had been discovered—derelict, on the farthest edges of town, and just inside their jurisdiction. Only, whereas the first location had been in the midst of undeveloped land, the newest scene was located among several buildings that had been shut down and abandoned long ago.

Several other cars were parked along the street, one of which was a news van. So it had hit that point already—the news was all over this, no doubt spurred on by what was starting to seem like an interdepartmental rivalry of sorts. She surveyed the scene and saw that there was a thin line of activity heading into a small alley between an old brick building and a smaller building that looked to have once been a convenience store.

She passed by two officers—one was Finley and the other was a younger guy she had never spoken to—keeping the press away from the alleyway. She edged by them and made her way into the alley. She saw O'Malley, Connelly, and Ramirez standing in a semicircle, all looking down.

She also saw Agent Duggan from the FBI. He barely looked up as she approached. He had apparently gotten the hint that she really didn't want his help. Still, she had to admit that the presence of the FBI made her feel a little more at ease. It showed that a case that was so far escaping her was severe enough to have the bureau involved.

When the four men heard her approach, O'Malley turned to her and nodded her over. She approached slowly, not liking the look on O'Malley's face. She cast her eyes to the ground and felt herself stop breathing for a few moments as she saw the body.

She could only *wish* this one had been reduced to nothing more than ash. As it was, though, this body had been only partially burned and that was somehow worse.

First of all, the shape of the actual body remained. While it was little more than bare bones from the waist down, flesh still clung to the abdomen, ribs, and lower neck. Even the lower half of the face remained and that, as far as Avery was concerned, was the most grisly thing of all, looking to a corner of a singed mouth that was

90

burned into a frown. What remained there was clearly skin and tissue but it had been badly charred.

"The damned thing still feels like there's heat coming off of it," O'Malley said. He then looked to Avery and Ramirez, giving them a hopeful and slightly angry look. "If you two could wrap this one up pronto, I'd appreciate it. We can't keep having this happen…especially not with the media on our heels and *you*," he said, stabbing a finger in Avery's directions, "setting out to make us look like idiots at every turn."

Agent Duggan looked at her with an amused little smile. Whatever respect he'd had for her when they first met seemed to be long gone.

"What the hell is that supposed to mean?" Avery asked.

"You were very vocal about Denny Cox being innocent," O'Malley said. "Simmons and the other B3 guys hung on your every word. And now that Cox is clean and off the hook, it's making us look like fools."

Maybe if you'd listened to me from the start, she thought, but bit the comment back. Instead, she slowly stalked around the scene, taking in every detail as she came to it. The first and most obvious thing to note was that this body was not nearly as burned down as the others has been.

He's either getting lazy or he was in a hurry this time, she thought.

With a grimace, she hunkered down next to the body. This one was also a female. She'd been burned with her clothes on; a few stray scraps of burned fabric were in her hair and fused to her chest. She looked at the woman's face. The flesh here had been totally burned away. Avery could see around the teeth, though, that a few traces of the gum line remained. She wondered if this might be enough for Sandy and her crew down in Forensics to mine some more information about when the burning had occurred.

She scoured the area for more fragments like they had found at the first scene but could find none. There were also no clearly visible footprints of any kind.

"What are you thinking?" Connelly asked her.

"I'm wondering why he did a sloppy job this time. I wonder if he intentionally left her in this state just to shock us or if he was hurried or rushed this time. Seeing the body like this makes me think he might not be as methodical as we originally thought."

"Great insights," Duggan said. Avery thought he was only speaking because he felt he needed to in order to be noticed. "If the killer has the capacity to be sloppy, he can screw up enough to basically leave a sign for us, making him easy to catch."

"A good theory, Black," O'Malley said. "Now let's see you prove it."

Avery continued to scour the area, looking for any sign as to how long the body had been there. She saw no clear drag marks, indicating that the killer had carried the body and then quite literally dumped it here in the alley. Her mind turned to the street corners out along the street. While this was a mostly dead part of the city, she thought the traffic cameras in the nearby stoplights might be worth checking out.

She was dimly aware of a cell phone ringing behind her and O'Malley's voice answering the call. His voice was agitated but she paid it very little mind as she continued to look around the alleyway.

No blood, no footprints...but maybe the lazy nature of the burn this time around will reveal some fingerprints or other damning evidence. Maybe—

"Black!"

She wheeled around at the sound of her shouted name. It had come from O'Malley and when she faced him, she saw absolute rage in his eyes. She also saw that he was still holding his cell phone. She wondered what the call had been about.

He stalked toward hers, leaving the other three men behind. Duggan watched on, clearly quite interested. When O'Malley reached her, they were nearly standing nose-to-nose. He spoke quietly but with unmistakable fury.

"What is it?" she asked.

"I just got a call from Peggy Stiller. You know who that is?"

"I can't say that I do."

"She's one of the security administrators over at South Bay House of Corrections. She and I go way back to when she was a lowly secretary for the local PD. The last time you got busted going to see that psycho Howard Randall, I called in a favor. I asked her to let me know if you ever showed your face over there again to speak with him. And guess what little bit of news I just received?"

"Sir, I—"

"Please correct me if I'm wrong. But after last time, didn't I specifically ask you to stop associating with Randall?"

"You did."

"So you agree that this would be considered insubordination, yes?"

He was nearly shouting now, attracting even the attention of Finley and the other officer who were still keeping the press away at the mouth of the alley. Duggan was also listening more intently than ever.

"Well?" O'Malley asked.

"Yes, I suppose so," Avery said.

O'Malley was fuming, doing everything he could not to lose his cool. He paced back and forth, looking from the burned body and then back to Avery. Apparently, he noticed that he was on the verge of causing a scene and lowered his voice again.

"Why'd you go see him this time?"

It was a simple question but the answer wasn't simple at all. She also knew that it was not an answer O'Malley wanted to hear. Still, there was no sense in playing dumb or trying to throw him off. "He's a resource," she said. "My past with him makes him one of the best resources at our disposal."

"Your past with him?" O'Malley roared. "Don't even get me *started* on your past with him. You know what, Black? I might regret this later but right now I just don't give a shit. I want you *off* of this case effective immediately. I can't stand for this sort of insubordination—especially when my orders were fairly well known throughout the A1."

"You can't be serious," Avery said.

"Oh, I am. You're damned good at what you do but you have to follow the rules the same as anyone else. And as a matter of fact, you've netted zero results on this one so far. I'll put Agent Duggan with Ramirez and work with them to wrap it up."

"Sir, you can't—"

But he had already turned his back to her. The only other thing he said was "Dismissed," before getting on the phone again.

She knew she could make a scene and argue her point further. But she knew O'Malley well enough to know when not to push it. So instead, she figured she'd take the high road. That way she could perhaps talk some sense into him tomorrow after things had calmed down. And she certainly didn't want to seem like a sniveling brat in front of a fed.

She turned her back on the scene and headed back for her car. When she passed by the reporters and the officers trying to keep them back, one of them asked her for information. It took everything in her to not wheel around on them and flip them off. She made it to her car and just as she was about to get in, Ramirez came rushing past the reporters and to her car.

"That's it?" Ramirez asked. "You're going to quit just like that?"

"I'm not quitting," she pointed out. "I'm following orders."

"Well, if they're going to take you off of the case, I'll step off of it, too," he said.

She was a little surprised by the offer given the way she had spoken to him yesterday but then again, that was just the kind of man Ramirez was. She sighed and shook her head. "No," she said. "Don't. This is *your* time to shine. See what you can do with this without me. Hell, you're going to have a federal agent as a partner."

"Yeah, sure...but O'Malley can't just throw you out like that."

"He can. And he has a right to do it. I fucked up. I get it and I understand it. But I know O'Malley. One more day and I'll give him a call. He'll cool down and come to his senses."

Ramirez hesitantly nodded his head and stepped back toward the alley. "Are you going to be okay?"

"Of course I am. Now get to work."

He grinned at her as she got into her car and pulled back out onto the street. Seeing him smile at her warmed her heart in spite of the way the morning had gone. She thought she might also need to give Ramirez a call tomorrow when things cooled down.

She turned around, trying to think of how to spend the rest of her day. Of course she wasn't going to just sit on her heels and do nothing. She was going to keep working on the case under the radar...but how?

Ahead of her and to the left, she saw a faint cloud of smoke drifting up into the sky. She followed it down and saw a thin smokestack, probably attached to the rear of a factory or mill on the eastern side of town.

This sparked an idea in her mind. Even before it had fully developed, she pulled up the number for the coroner. She didn't want to bother with calling anyone at A1; if O'Malley found out, he'd be livid. It would take him a little longer to figure out that she had contacted the coroner, though.

She made the call and was relieved when the receptionist didn't ask for her name. All she said was that she was calling with the A1 and she was put through. Then after two minutes or so, the phone was picked up on the other end.

"How can I help you guys?" the coroner asked in a tired voice.

"Well, as you know, we're up to our necks in trying to figure out this recent case with burned bodies," she said. "I'm putting together a list of places in the city other than morgues and crematoriums that include burning and fires in their line of work."

"Well, there's paper mills," the coroner said, "but the heat generated in those places wouldn't be nearly strong enough. There's steel mills, but there are only two in the city and one of them has such rigid security that it would be impossible for someone to get in and out. The other one has been shut down for about six months. The only other place might be a garbage-burning plant. There's one of those in town and it stays pretty busy."

"Garbage burning?" Avery asked. "Would that process generate enough heat to burn a body to ash?"

"If it was exposed long enough."

"Are we talking temperatures of one thousand degrees or more?"

"No idea, lady. You'd have to talk to someone at the plant. Sorry, but I never got your name…what did you say it was?"

She killed the call and looked back to the rising cloud of smoke in the distance. She pulled up the address to Boston's single garbage-burning plant and when she viewed it on the map, she studied it carefully. From first glance, the plant appeared to be exactly in the middle of the triangle of where the bodies had been discovered.

She pulled an illegal U-turn at the next light and was following the GPS directions within thirty seconds.

CHAPTER TWENTY ONE

The stink of the garbage-burning plant was awful but not nearly as bad as she had expected. By the time she had parked her car, walked across the lot and into the central office, she had almost gotten used to it. It smelled more like burning plastic than anything else, with a sort of spoiled and rotten undertone to it.

She'd called ahead to speed things up so when she stepped into the front office, there was an older gentleman waiting for her. His name was Ned Armstrong and he worked as the shift director. When he smiled at her when she entered, he looked very happy to be doing something other than his usual job.

"Thanks for meeting with me," Avery said.

"Of course," Ned said. "This is actually the perfect time to give you a quick tour of the place if you'd like. The peak burn time is about two hours from now, when most of the trucks have come back from their routes."

"Perfect," Avery said. "Lead the way."

"On the phone, you said you were more interested in the area where we burn material, correct?"

"Yes. Or, more directly, we're looking to see if this facility has the capacity to burn bodies without the knowledge of supervisors."

"Well, I can assure you there's nothing like that going on around here," he said. "Come on and I'll take you to the compacting and burn center. You'll see what I mean."

Being something of an information junkie, Avery was rather glad to find that the compacting and burn center was at the back of the building. Along the way, she was able to see most of the day-to day-operations of the plant. Ned pointed things out here and there but Avery was able to get the gist of just about everything on her own.

They passed by a large concrete square of a room where trucks backed in and out. From there, the garbage was sorted and then carried further into the facility on a series of forklifts. There were other rooms where some heavily soiled materials such as heavy plastics, metals, and aluminum were cleansed and re-sorted. All of this then led to the back of the building, where Ned finally showed her the compacting and burning quarters.

"I think this is what you'd be most interested to see," Ned said as he led her inside the room.

To the right, there were three machines that Ned called balers. They were short and long, all capped with a large iron door. She and Ned watched as a worker filled one of the balers with an assortment of materials that were all unrecyclable. This included what looked like ripped couch cushions, badly damaged plastic, some sort of old molded wood, and scraps of chicken wire among other unnamable things.

The worker shoved all of this material into the baler, using a simple tool that looked almost like a shovel with a flat head to cram it all in. When it was packed in, he closed the iron door and locked it with a large bolt. He then ran a series of three large wires through the balers, using small holes drilled into the side. With these wires in place, he then turned on a hydraulic press that pushed all of the material inside up against the bolted door. Avery could not see the effect of the press but she could hear the rending and tearing of the materials inside.

Thirty seconds later, the press was done and retracted. When it was over, the worker popped the door open and pressed a green button along the side of the baler. A loud beeping sounded out as a mechanism inside the baler pushed out a nearly perfectly square-shaped bale of material. It was about three feet high and six feet wide—all of the detritus that had just been shoved in pressed down and tied with wires in a neat bundle.

"We then take these bales to the burn center," Ned said. "We recycle everything we can but as you might imagine, not everything that comes through here is able to be recycled."

He led her through a large garage-type door beside them, leading them into another concrete room. Several bales similar to the one she had just seen were sitting to the far right of the room. The back of the room consisted of what looked like a very large baler. But the fact that she could feel the heat of it and smell the burning scent of plastic and other materials clued her in to what she was really seeing.

"This is where it's all burned?" she asked.

"Yes. Every now and then we'll get a piece of metal or something that is too big to go in there. We put those to the side and ship them off to the steel mill. We don't get a lot of it, though. We gather them all up in shipments and send them off. We might get enough to send out a single shipment every year."

"And do you ever get anything...unusual?"

"Oh yeah. We get dead animals all the time. Cats, dogs, raccoons. It's gross."

"And what do you do with them?"

"It's annoying, actually. We burn them separately, so it can really slow a shift down."

"Have you ever found a body in the garbage?" Avery asked.

"No. But last year we did find two toes and a finger. Called the police in and everything, but nothing ever came of it."

Avery watched as two bales were placed into the burner. There was nothing fancy about it at all. It served very much as a furnace; a large front door was opened, clanging open much like the baler door. The bales were inserted via a miniature forklift and then the door was closed. An operator hit two switches and they could all hear the roaring of the fire as it blasted what had been placed inside.

"What's the temperature get to in there?" she asked.

"Around eight hundred degrees. Sometimes it'll get as high as one thousand, but that comes down to what's inside the bale that we put in."

"And I assume there's a certain amount of background checks and training that goes into hiring someone for this job?" Avery asked.

"Absolutely...especially for the baler and the burner. You've got to be a quick thinker when operating these things. If something were to go wrong with the burner, for instance, it has to be shut down and fixed pretty quickly. If that fire keeps going for more than forty-five minutes, it can start doing internal damage."

"Have you ever had to fire anyone that worked back here?"

"Me personally, no. But there's a pretty widespread story from about seven years ago. I was working in sorting then. Apparently, the guy that was working the baler and the guy working the burner got into a little accident with the lifts. This was right before the burner was cleaned, so all of the cleaning supplies were out, you know? One of the lifts knocked some of them over and one of the guys fell right in it."

"What were the chemicals?" Avery asked. "Were they harmful?"

"All I can remember for sure are acetone, amine, and oxide. Stuff that's hard to pronounce, much less memorize. He got some chemical burns on his face and hands and a few days later started to act sort of odd. I think there was always speculation that it was because of the chemicals. But no one ever really fussed much about it. Still, after a month or so of him acting irrational and weird, he was fired."

"Weird how?"

"I don't know myself," he said. "From what I hear, he would just lash out at people. He started to get a little too interested in cleaning the burner. He *loved* the chemicals used for cleaning it...really started to get obsessed with it."

"Are his records in human resources?" Avery asked.

"Sure thing. I can fetch them for you if you like."

Ned led her back out of the burner room but before she left back through the large door, she looked back at the burner. She tried to think about a person being trapped in something like that as fire leaped up around them.

Trapped…the heat growing more intense…no escape.

Despite the visions of fire and heat within her head, Avery couldn't help but shudder.

CHAPTER TWENTY TWO

Avery pulled up in front of the residence of George Lutz a little over an hour later. Without an official capacity to use A1 resources at her own disposal, she'd had to call Ramirez and have him hunt down more information based on the records HR had given her at the trash plant. All in all, she knew that Lutz had been fired four years ago and since then had managed to work as a fry cook at Wendy's before being let go from there as well. Medical tests and psych evaluations had deemed him fit for society but unable to hold a steady job; he was therefore living on government assistance in a low-income house that had been paid for by his aunt.

The house was surprisingly well maintained. The small square of a porch looked to have been freshly painted and the windows were so clean they were sparkling. The grass was mown almost exquisitely—but that was also where Avery saw the first signs of just how far George Lutz had fallen since the days of his accident at the trash-firing plant.

There was a huge assortment of lawn ornaments surrounding the house. There were pink flamingos, garden gnomes, and ceramic mushrooms. And they were *everywhere*. In fact, as Avery stepped out of her car, she saw a man sitting on the edge of the lawn, facing one of the gnomes. He was holding a small canister of paint and touching up a red pair of suspenders on the gnome's ceramic body.

"Excuse me," Avery said. "Are you George Lutz?"

The man froze for a moment and then finished his current swab of paint before turning to face her. He had a thick unkempt beard and scraggly hair that was mostly tucked under a driver's cap. He looked a little off his rocker but in an almost childlike way.

"Sure am," he said. "Who are you?"

"My name is Avery Black," she said. "I work for the police."

"Oh," he said, dropping his paintbrush and turning to face her.

She saw that she had guessed right. Whatever was wrong with him made him seem very much like a child. It was her assumption of this that had made her keep her description very basic. *I work for the police* was going to be a lot more interesting to a child than *I'm a detective with the Boston A1 Homicide division.*

"Am I in trouble?" Lutz asked.

"No," she said. "But I've been looking into some things going on down at the trash plant you used to work at. I was wondering if you could answer some questions about it."

Lutz nodded, but frowned. "I don't really like that place. They were mean to me there."

"How so?"

"They fired me because of the accident. They said I wasn't doing my job right anymore."

Avery had read all about the incidents that had occurred after the accident. George had complained of headaches and missed quite a few days. And when he *had* reported for work, he'd goofed off most of the time and had created an unsafe working environment for everyone he came in contact with. He'd also been caught starting fires in the burner that had absolutely nothing to do with his work. That had been the final straw that had lost him his job.

"Yeah, I understand you had some headaches back then or something," Avery said as she walked closer to him, trying to seem sympathetic. She looked down at the garden gnomes and realized that there was something almost morbidly comical about them— about this entire situation, in fact.

"I did," Lutz said. "But not anymore. I'm taking medicine for them."

"I see," Avery said. "But tell me, please…I also hear that you got in trouble for starting small fires in the burner. Is that right?"

"Yeah," Lutz said.

"Why were you doing that?"

Lutz shifted uncomfortably. He picked up his paintbrush and absently dipped it into his paint. "I was only trying to understand it. The fire, I mean. I don't know…it's pretty. Well, it *was*."

"And it's not anymore?"

Lutz shook his head and raised his left arm. She looked at his hand and saw scarring along the palm and last two fingers. They were very bad burns that had not healed very well.

"No," he said. "Now it's scary. I don't like it. So I just paint now. I like mixing it and repainting my yard friends."

"I see," Avery said and with that, she was certain that George Lutz was not the killer. He did not have the capacity for such a thing. And although she was far from a psychologist, she recognized his fear of fire as a real thing. He had trembled slightly when showing her his burns.

"So you've had no more trouble with headaches or starting fires?" Avery asked.

"Nope. I still think fire can be pretty…but it's too mean. It breaks stuff. Destroys stuff. Think about house fires and forest fires. Did you know that sometimes when people die, their families will burn them? That's…messed up. Why would you do that?"

Avery made a *hmm* sound of agreement. But her mind was elsewhere. She was thinking of urns and crematoriums…and broken fragments of a ceramic or glass urn at the first site where they had found the body of Keisha Lawrence.

When she had spoken with Sandy Ableton, the dental forensics expert, Avery had realized that crematoriums might be worth looking into but probably were not a priority.

Maybe I was wrong, she thought. *I overlooked it because it was too obvious. But after the trash plant and speaking to poor George Lutz…everything is pointing in that direction.*

"Well, George…thank you for your time. I'll leave you to your painting."

"Would you like to join me?" Lutz asked. "I've got to paint this guy and all of his friends. They're getting filthy out here."

"Thanks for the invitation, but no," Avery said. "I need to get going."

Lutz gave her a simple little nod before turning back to his work. She barely saw it, as she was lost in thought.

The urns, she thought. *The broken urn fragments…that should have been a dead give-away. Did I overthink this one?*

George Lutz was still painstakingly working on the same set of suspenders when Avery pulled her car away from the curb and pulled up directions for the closest crematorium.

CHAPTER TWENTY THREE

The ash and burn smears were cleaned away and his chamber was clean again. Something had gone wrong with the last one and he'd had to extinguish the fire before the body had been completely burned. He wasn't sure if it had to do with the ventilation of the chamber or something he had done wrong while starting the fire. Whatever it had been, the end result had been grisly and gruesome. He wasn't about to let that happen again.

He had installed an additional layer of mineral wool behind the panels. He had also created several mats of wicker, which he had discovered several years ago was one of the most highly combustible household materials available that would go undetected in lab tests. That's why he tended to stay away from liquid accelerants. He always used a bit of propane to get things started, preferring it over gasoline because it was harder to detect in tests. Sometimes he'd use a standard tin of lighter fluid, something he usually kept on hand at the edge of his desk.

He held the tin now, as he stared into the chamber. With the chamber ready to go, he peered into the box of materials he had prepared for the next body. He thought he'd had the process perfect until that last body had been so terribly uncooperative. He assumed most people thought there was nothing to burning a body. Set a fire to it and be done with it.

But there was much more to it than that. There was a process—an *art* to it.

He looked into his box and counted out his materials for the sixth time. There was extra wicker and several sheets of foam insulation. The insulation was one of the most hazardous household accelerants…so much so that he had seen research where people selling home insurance had actually referred to it as "solid gasoline" and required other fail-safes for construction in order to offer affordable insurance rates.

With an itch of anticipation, he plucked one of the folded sheets of insulation from the box and carried it into the chamber. He laid it in the center of the chamber and then went to his small desk and retrieved a single Post-it note and a lighter. He folded the Post-it in quarters, spritzed it with a bit of lighter fluid from the can, and set it aflame with the lighter.

He carried the Post-it carefully to the chamber. When the little flames licked at his fingers he smiled. Yes, it stung…but it was a pleasant sting. He was giggling to himself as he finally reached the chamber.

He carefully plucked the burning Post-it into the chamber and quickly closed the door. By the time he had it bolted securely, he could hear the whisperlike *whoosh* of flame being born on the other side. He placed his hands against the door and imagined he could feel the heat already, the power of it trying to eat its way out.

He smiled as he listened to the growing flame and ran his hands sensually along the door. He waited for fifteen minutes, standing perfectly motionless against the door. He then carefully opened the door, reveling in the wave of heat that rushed out at him.

As he expected, the foam had been burned down to little more than dust. A few tufts of its original form remained but he knew they would also crumble to dust when he swept them out.

He had twenty-five more sheets of the foam, several handmade sheets of wicker, and an oil-based accelerant he had created himself that he would splash onto the victim. He had worked very hard before beginning his work to create a starter accelerant that was virtually untraceable. He wondered, perhaps, if he had been too lenient with the oil on the last victim; perhaps that was why she had not burned completely.

Whatever the reason, he had failed. And he had lived his life in a constant state of fear of failure. It was, he supposed, what had driven him to this point.

He took the single broom from the small closet on the right side of the room and swept the meager burnt offerings from the foam out of his chamber. He was meticulous, making sure he did not leave the slightest bit of ash.

When it was clean again, he stared into the chamber and wondered for an agonizing moment what it might be like to be inside while the fire was reaching its maximum strength. He peered into that empty and waiting space, wondering what it might be like to burn.

CHAPTER TWENTY FOUR

Avery was sitting in the waiting area of Wallace Funeral Home and Crematorium, doing her best not to feel too unsettled by the funeral parlor atmosphere. Due to her line of work, the fact and reality of death did not bother her. But ever since childhood, something about the idea of a place that was built only for the housing of the dead and their mourners had seemed eerie. It was a feeling that still haunted her even now.

With the way the day had gone, she was starting to feel almost like a tourist or a kid on some sort of morbid field trip. First a tour of a recycling and trash-burning center and now this. A few quick calls had bought her some time with the owner of Wallace Funeral Home and Crematorium. She had not spoken with him directly but a receptionist had set it all up.

Everything seemed to be happening quite fast now, as the door to the back of the building opened up. A man dressed in a tasteful gray suit entered the waiting room and gave her an uncertain smile.

"Detective Black?" he asked.

"Yes."

"Pleased to meet you. I'm Sawyer Wallace. I heard there was some pressing business I can help you with?"

Avery took a moment to go over the more minor details of the case, treading carefully as she was not sure what he had already seen on the news.

"I'm tracking down a suspect that is kidnapping his victims—all women, to this point—and burning them. He is burning them in a way that makes me think he really knows what he is doing. He's going right down to the bone in most cases. At each scene so far, there have been fragments of what looked to be broken urns."

With each detail she spilled, Wallace seemed to sit a little more upright in his seat. By the time Avery was done, he was as straight as a board and his eyes were wide with terror.

"That's absolutely horrible," Wallace said.

"Yes, it is. I was wondering what you could tell me about the cremation process...perhaps even show me the process in action."

"Well, it would take some paperwork for me to show you the process up close and personal," Wallace said. "But I can answer any questions you have."

He remained in the chair opposite her, a non-verbal way of letting her know that she would not be getting any further inside the building than the waiting room. And as far as Avery was concerned, that was fine with her. She was starting to feel almost as unsettled as Wallace looked.

"Well, I'd like to know if it would be at all possible for someone to burn a body quite efficiently somewhere other than a crematorium. I'm talking all the way down to nothing but ash and bone."

"Well," Wallace said, doing his best to act as if the news she had shared with him had not taken him off guard, "with cremations, of course, everything is reduced to ash. Bones and teeth are ground down to nothing more than powder. So if there is bone remaining in these remains, the killer is not achieving the same temperatures we are. The bones would at least get weaker and slightly broken down before we crush them. If he is not doing that or does not even have the option, I'd guess he is almost certainly not burning them for as long as a typical cremation, or at the same temperatures."

"But hypothetically, could it be done?"

Wallace thought about it for a moment before answering: "Yes, I suppose so. You'd need some sort of designated room, though. It would have to be built quite well and extremely fire resistant. And even then...it would almost *have* to be some sort of industrial building. If it wasn't, there's no way the structure would last very long."

"And how about chemicals?" Avery asked. "Are there any chemicals involved in the cremation process? We've caught a faint smell from the ash but nothing solid is coming up when we test it."

"No chemicals, just natural gases. Some crematoriums use a special kind of oil, but we don't do that here."

"But the process is basically the same at all crematoriums?"

"Yes, in America. Of course when you get overseas and into Eastern religions, there are a variety of practices."

"Well, I'd think we're looking for someone who has a strong interest in the process of burning things or starting fires—not an arsonist exactly, but someone who respects fire and maybe even is using it symbolically. So please forgive me for asking, but I was wondering if there was anyone in the crematorium's past that might have been a cause for concern. Anyone that was maybe fired or corrected for unusual behavior?"

"Fortunately, no," Wallace said. "Not here. But three years ago, there was a very troubling incident at one of the other crematoriums."

Now it was Avery's turn to sit up straight and take notice. *Here we go...*

"What sort of incident?" Avery asked.

Wallace shifted uncomfortably in his seat and eyed Avery uneasily. "I don't know that it would be proper for me to tell someone else's business," Wallace said.

"I respect that, but time is of the essence," Avery said. "Anything you can tell me will speed up the process while we seek out the employees of the other crematorium." What she left out was the fact that someone working for that crematorium might downplay the extremity of the event to save face.

Clearly uncomfortable, Wallace nodded. "There was a man working at the Peaceful Hills Crematorium that was not only released, but spent some time in a psych ward from what I understand. It started out when he was found sleeping on the graves of people that his parlor buried. That was more than enough reason for them to fire him—and they did. But after the fact, it was also discovered that he was secretly making videos of the cremations on his iPhone. Later, when the police looked through his computer, they found videos of war crimes where people were being burned. Close-up, gruesome stuff."

"Do you know the man's name?"

Wallace was still clearly not comfortable with sharing the information, but when he leaned forward in a secretive way, Avery knew that he was going to tell what he knew.

"Phillip Bailey. He worked for them for nearly four years before anyone caught on to his issues."

"And is he still being treated? Is he at a home of some kind?"

"No. He's living in town. And the only way I know this for sure is because he applied for a position here several months ago. I reported it to the authorities and I think he was basically given a little slap on the wrist and nothing more."

"He applied *here*?" Avery asked. "So you'd have his address on file?"

"I could have HR pull it, yes."

"It would be a huge help."

Wallace sighed and got to his feet. "One moment," he said, exiting back through the same door he had entered through.

When he was gone, Avery took out her phone. Before placing her call, she checked the time and saw that it had somehow come to be 3:10. It had been one of those days where she had somehow forgotten to grab lunch and was running on pure adrenaline (and a little bit of anger from having been technically removed from the case).

She then pulled up Ramirez's name and pressed CALL. She understood that there was some sort of irony to her calling him for help given the way she had been treating him over the last day or so—but they had both learned to put work ahead of their relationship and she figured this was no different.

As if to confirm this, he answered on the second ring. "Hey, Avery. Hard at work?"

"You know me too well."

"You're probably further ahead of the curve than I am right now. I'm getting nothing."

"Well, let me give you a little something then," she said. "I've been doing some digging and I'm about to get the contact information for what looks like a promising lead. Do you think you can meet up with me without O'Malley finding out?"

"Probably," Ramirez said. "I'm behind a desk right now. I'm pretty sure he'd like to see me moving around instead of just sitting here. And our buddy Agent Duggan skipped out about an hour ago, heading back to his office in Chelsea."

"Has O'Malley cooled down at all yet?" Avery asked.

"A little. Just stressed. This latest body is really getting to him. If the media had has seen the state of it…"

"Yeah, I know. Look, can you meet me in an hour?"

"Just tell me where."

She did, giving him a rendezvous point a few blocks away. When they ended the call, things felt almost the way they had before they had slept together three nights ago. She wasn't sure if that was a good thing or a bad thing, though. It *felt* like a good thing but there was also something a little sad about it.

Seconds later, Wallace walked back out. He held out a piece of paper to her and Avery saw that it was a photocopy of Phillip Bailey's application.

"I do hope you can catch and stop whoever is doing this. But if it comes down to it and it *is* Phillip Bailey, I'd much rather you leave my name out of it."

"Of course," Avery said. "And thank you for your help."

Wallace gave her a quick handshake and then once again returned through the door and out of the waiting area. Avery checked the application for an address and found that it would be about a twenty-minute drive from where she currently was. She toyed with the idea of calling Ramirez again and simply giving him the address to meet her there.

But if she was flying under the radar, trying to stay out of O'Malley's way, she needed to play it safe. She pocketed the application and headed back out to her car. She again found herself thinking of fire, of how it was the perfect way to get rid of something—of *anything*, really. And, beyond that, she thought of the sort of person that would be depraved enough to use it as a way to end a human life and was rather glad she had decided to call Ramirez.

CHAPTER TWENTY FIVE

It was 4:47 when Avery and Ramirez pulled up to the residence of Phillip Bailey. As Avery parked the car, Ramirez was getting off the phone with someone from records at the A1. When he ended the call, he looked out to the house on their right and nodded his head.

"Well, his record sure as hell checks out. This guy is a creep, all right. According to the reports, there was one thing that Wallace left out of the story about Bailey sleeping on those graves."

"What's that?"

"He was mostly naked and when they found him, he was...well, he was *aroused*."

"Well, if this guy *isn't* the one we're looking for, it seems like he's certainly worth looking into," Avery said. "Especially if he is actively trying to get jobs at crematoriums."

"You sure you don't want me to call this in?" Ramirez asked. "This guy is straight up spooky if you ask me."

"No, not until we know for sure. If I'm wrong on this, it could be my ass."

With a shared look that was filled with far too much emotion and anxiousness to make sense of, Avery and Ramirez opened their doors and stepped out onto the street. Bailey's house was a modest-looking home, complete with a rickety porch swing hanging from old chains.

They came up to the front door quietly, seeing that the door was open, leaving the house protected by only a flimsy screen door. As they approached, Avery could hear the slight murmur of a television from inside. Elsewhere, very faintly, she could hear muted tapping noises. It sounded almost as if someone was hammering something from within the house.

Avery knocked on the screen door and waited for a response but all there was to hear was the TV. It sounded like it was tuned to a late-afternoon talk show. Then, after ten seconds or so, the tapping noise sounded again. This time, it was louder. Almost violent.

Avery knocked once more, louder this time. The screen door rattled, drowning out the television. "Phillip Bailey?" she called through the screen door.

Almost immediately, the tapping sound stopped.

"Was that hammering?" Ramirez asked quietly.

Avery shrugged and then called through the door. "I'm looking for Phillip Bailey. This is a police matter."

There was still no response. Avery thought things out and wondered if perhaps she should have remained quiet. She looked to Ramirez and said, "Head around back to see if there's a back door or cellar he could leave through. If I don't see you in twenty seconds, I'm going to assume there *is* a back way and you're standing by it. At that point, I'm going in."

Ramirez gave a nod, hurried down the stairs, and sprinted around the side of the house. Avery turned her attention back to the screen door and started counting. As she did, she peered into the house through the screen door.

The place was a bit of a mess. A small coffee table was littered with papers and magazines. A laptop sat on a small couch that was cluttered with more paper, a plate with half of a sandwich, and several crumpled paper towels. Further back, she could see part of a hallway, but little else.

When she reached twenty seconds in her head, she knocked once more, waited, and then opened the screen door. She stepped in and saw that the TV was indeed tuned to an afternoon talk show. She went to the laptop on the couch and saw what looked to be a resume in progress. At the bottom of the screen, along the task bar, she saw the Google Chrome icon. She pulled it up and saw that whoever had been using it was logged into a career website.

She stepped away from it and started toward the hallway.

That's when the smell hit her.

It was ghastly, like being slapped in the face with the carcass of an animal that had been rotting on the side of the road. It was so powerful that Avery took a step back and held her breath. Making a conscious effort to breathe through her mouth, Avery continued down the hallway. To her right, a small kitchen opened up to reveal a surprisingly clean counter and sink. A bowl of fruit sat decoratively on a tiny kitchen table.

The smell was not coming from here. More importantly, she noticed that the sounds of faint hammering had stopped as soon as she had come inside the house. If Phillip Bailey was here, he apparently knew that he was not alone now.

She nearly called out again but if he *was* inside, there was no sense in purposefully giving herself away. She continued down the hallway. Every door she passed was open, revealing a bathroom, a bedroom, and a cluttered study. Inside the study, another laptop glowed from a tattered desk otherwise littered with books.

Her instincts told her she'd find answers in there but right now, she was more worried about locating Phillip Bailey. She turned away from the office and started forward again. The hall came to an end ahead of her, but not before one more door broke up the hallway to her left. It was closed, but light shined through the cracks along the bottom and the sides.

She reached for the handle, turned it, and was surprised to find that it opened. She pulled it open and found herself staring not only at a set of stairs that led down into a basement, but at a man standing on those stairs.

He was startled, but also looked as if he had been caught doing something. She assumed he had been creeping up the stairs as she had been investigating the house, hoping to get the drop on her.

"Are you Phillip Bailey?" she asked.

"I am," he said. "Who the hell are you?"

Before she answered, she made a show of slowly reaching for her sidearm. She started to answer him but then saw his hands. They were covered in something that was either black or very dark red.

"I'm Detective Avery Black with the Boston Police," she said. "Homicide."

Bailey looked confused at first but then smiled. "Really?"

"What's on your hands, Mr. Bailey?"

He looked to his hands as if he hadn't known there was anything on them. As he studied them, Avery was very much aware that the smell that had nearly bowled her over earlier seemed to be coming from below the stairs.

"Would you believe paint?" he asked.

"Mr. Bailey," she said, drawing her gun. "I'm going to ask you to lift your hands in the air, turn around, and lead me into the basement."

"We don't need to do that," Bailey said.

"Oh, I think we do. Do it now, Mr. Bailey." She then leaned her head to the left and gave a quick shout. "Ramirez! Come on in!"

With a sigh of defeat, Bailey did as he was asked. When he did, Avery saw more of the black or dark red substance on his shirt.

That's blood, she thought. *No way in hell that's* not *blood.*

She followed Bailey down the stairs. The smell grew stronger and she started to realize that it was two separate things she was smelling. The first was of something very much like the smell a dead animal leaves on the side of the road.

The other was the unmistakable smell of smoke and something that had been badly burned.

We got the bastard, she thought. *I can't believe it was this easy, but we—*

But when she reached the basement floor and looked to Phillip Bailey's grisly work area, she wasn't so sure.

She had been right: Phillip Bailey had been worth checking out. He might not be guilty of the recent deaths they were investigating, but he was certainly guilty of *something.*

Behind her, Ramirez came down the stairs. "Everything okay down h—?"

But his words were cut off when his eyes fell on the same scene Avery was trying to understand. He then found his words, changing his question.

"What the fuck?"

Phillip Bailey looked at them rather dumbly and then back down to his blood-streaked hands. "Shit," he said. "Am I in trouble?"

Neither of them answered. They were too busy trying to make sense of what they were seeing.

On a large oak table covered in a tarp, the body of a large cat was split open from neck to stomach. There was surprisingly little blood, as the incision looked neat. Beside the cat, a small Tupperware dish contained the contents of the cat, again surprisingly tidy and well tended to.

On the floor, pushed against the wall, there were several large coolers. Avery stepped toward them. Beside her, Phillip Bailey took a step forward.

"Nope," Ramirez said, aiming his gun at Bailey. "You don't move."

"The cat on the table is a stray," Bailey said, as if it explained everything. "I don't think it had an owner. No one will miss it."

Avery barely heard any of this as she peered into the fist cooler. She gagged a bit when she saw the contents. Inside was another cat. This one had not been gutted but had been burned quite badly. Its head was little more than a skull. Rotted black tissue was exposed along its ribs. Next to the cat was what looked to have once been a gerbil or guinea pig. Currently, though, it was little more than a black and pink charred ball with legs.

"Jesus," Avery said, fumbling for her phone to call it in.

This gruesome find actually made her quite sure that Phillip Bailey was not their killer, but the maniac needed to be locked up regardless.

"You can't call," Ramirez reminded her. "Let me do it."

She nodded as she looked into the next cooler. There, she found a medium-sized dog that had been partially burned, along with two more cats. She scanned the room and saw a small rack with other tarps and plastic sheeting. There was a can of gasoline, too. On the floor there were slight maroon stains, indicating that Bailey had been at this for quite some time.

She listened to Ramirez call it in while she turned slowly toward Bailey. She did all she could to keep her voice level and calm. She flicked the barrel of her Glock toward the stairs. "Lead me upstairs."

He sighed, as if this was a massive inconvenience, but did as he was asked.

Upstairs, she checked every room as Bailey led the way. Ramirez joined her, making the search go a bit faster. When she went to the laptop in the room she supposed served as a study, she pulled up the browser and checked Bailey's internet history. She was looking for any sort of evidence of Bailey having looked for the correct way to burn a human body, but found nothing.

What she *did* find was every single one of the videos he took while working at the crematorium. She also saw where he had watched a few YouTube videos of cremations, even ones from Nepal where they burned the bodies of deceased loved ones on a river near religious temples. There was also the entire video of the concert fire back in the '90s when the one-hit wonder rock group Great White shot off pyros and just about everyone at the venue burned alive.

She wasn't sure how long they searched the house maybe ten minutes. When the first police car arrived by that time, she wasted no time in heading outside. She barely heard Ramirez update the officers as she took a seat on Phillip Bailey's front steps.

After a few moments, Ramirez sat with her as they both listened to the commotion from inside the house. Avery was trying her best to make sense of what they had found in the basement but she was also waiting for O'Malley to bring the hammer down on her. He had not arrived at the scene yet but she was pretty sure he'd blow a fuse when he did. She could have easily split the scene when Ramirez had called it in but decided that was the coward's way out. This was her find and Ramirez was her partner. She'd stick with him through this, not to take the credit for the discovery but to take the fall for it if they turned out to be wrong.

Avery breathed in the fresh air of a gathering dusk.

"What the hell is wrong with people?" Ramirez asked.

"That's a loaded question," Avery said.

One of the officers who had first arrived stepped out onto the porch. He looked a little pale in the face, but determined.

"The creep is still down in the basement," he said. "He hasn't asked for a lawyer yet even though he's essentially under arrest. You need anything else out of him?"

It took Ramirez a moment to realize that the officer was speaking to him, not Avery. He seemed to be having trouble remembering that Avery was, as of right now, not officially on the case.

"No. Book him and take him in."

The officer nodded and turned back into the house. Avery and Ramirez remained on the porch steps. Avery badly wanted him to put an arm around her but he remained professional.

"You okay?" he asked.

"Yeah. That was just…unexpected."

"I'll say. I don't think I'll ever—"

A car pulled up across the street, coming to a shuddering stop. They both recognized it at once. They fell into silence yet again when O'Malley stepped out. He saw them sitting on the stairs, honed in on Avery, and shook his head in frustration.

"This should be fun," Ramirez joked as O'Malley came marching across the street. "You mind if I stick around and watch the shit hit the fan?"

"Please do," she said with a smirk, and she got to her feet to meet O'Malley.

CHAPTER TWENTY SIX

As night settled in and word of Phillip Bailey's arrest filtered through the A1, the headquarters started to smell of freshly brewed coffee and an overworked Xerox machine. Avery was starting on her second cup of coffee of the night as the members of a late and hastily thrown together meeting concerning the arrest filed into the conference room.

A sense of closure was starting to fill the room as everyone was under the impression that although there was no definitive proof, Phillip Bailey was the man they were looking for. There were still questions, of course, but the severity of what they had found in Bailey's basement seemed to line up with most of what they had expected to find in a killer. Even Avery was unable to get the sight from her mind and the smell from her nose.

Avery didn't think it quite fit, though. In the same way the childlike manner of George Lutz had not aligned with what she was looking for in a killer, there was something about Phillip Bailey that didn't quite fit, either. There was something about the nearly aloof way he had reacted to being caught that didn't sit right with her.

Am I in trouble?

He'd asked the question as if the whole thing had been a laughing matter. But the way the bodies they had found had been dispersed made her think that there was nothing playful about their killer. The carefree attitude Bailey was showing didn't seem to line up with the personality she was expecting their killer to have.

In other words, she felt that they had busted someone that certainly did not belong in society, but she didn't feel that Phillip Bailey was responsible for the deaths of Keisha Lawrence, Sarah Osborne, and the as-of-yet unidentified third victim.

Even if he'd started working up his nerve with humans, there was no way he could have burned bodies in that basement. Wallace even said that someone doing such a thing would need a dedicated room or building for such a thing.

Her thoughts were broken as O'Malley took the floor in his usual way—like a concerned father that was doing everything he could not to vent all of his anger and frustration out over his kids. She was relieved to see, though, that he looked mostly happy. She assumed this was because he was also under the impression that they had nailed their killer.

"First and foremost," O'Malley said, "Black is back on this case. So as we wrap it all up, everyone defer to her. Got it?"

A few murmurs of agreement trickled across the table. Some of those in attendance rolled their eyes in disbelief. It was a look Avery had long ago gotten used to.

"I hear you, trust me," O'Malley said. "But in a case like this, I'm willing to overlook her direct opposition of my orders, seeing as how she managed to do in one day what our entire department could not—bring in this guy. Now...he's being questioned and we've got a small Forensics team scouring his house for other proof. As of about ten minutes ago, we've also discovered several scattered bones buried in his backyard but they are almost certainly the remains of a large dog."

"Are we still lacking evidence to point towards the use of humans in his little experiments?" Avery asked.

"So far, yes. And damn it, Black...don't you dare go doubting me on this. You nailed this bastard and I've put you back on task. Don't butt heads with me on this."

"Yes sir," she said reluctantly.

O'Malley sighed and placed his hands on his hips. "For the sake of argument, Black, what are your concerns?"

"My concerns are that if he *is* our guy, he wasn't burning human bodies in his home. Torching a cat in a cooler is one thing. But you're not going to be able to burn a human body in a cooler, sir. If this is our guy, he's got another location somewhere and I think we should be putting our time and resources into finding it."

O'Malley nodded in an appreciative way. "I want a team on that right now," he said, looking around the table. "But as of right now, all signs are pointing this being our guy. Further digging shows that he also tried getting jobs at two other crematoriums in the city. He also attempted to take classes at the community college dealing with human anatomy but failed out after one semester. There were trace amounts of gasoline in the lining of those coolers, which shows he has no problem keeping the necessary materials on hand. Two plus two equals four, people. Sometimes we get lucky and it all matches up. Damn good work, Black. You too, Ramirez."

More eye rolls and a brief smattering of reluctant applause filled the room. Avery looked to Ramirez, who gave her a sly little grin.

"That's it," O'Malley said. "It's late and we need to get feelers out for a second location this creep was using. Break, people! Get to work."

The small crowd got up from the conference room table and disbanded. As Avery tried to do the same, Connelly stepped in front of her. "One second, Black."

She stepped to the side as the last of the attendees filed out. Ramirez hung behind, remaining in his seat. "Do I need to go?" he asked.

"No, you're her partner," O'Malley said, joining Connelly. "You should probably hear this, too."

He closed the door and took a seat at the conference room table. Connelly joined him and the two men shared a brief glance that Avery could not read. A thick and uncomfortable silence filled the room, making Avery feel like she was on trial for something.

"Here's the deal, Black," O'Malley said. "Yes, you disobeyed me yet again today. But you also managed to get stellar results without anyone's help. We understand that Ramirez came to your side, which technically puts him on my shit list but I'm willing to overlook it. Black…I don't even know what to do with you. The results you bring in time and time again can't be ignored. And the fact that you were on your own today and got more done than our entire department shows that you don't mind going it alone. And Ramirez…you complement her well. You could have taken full credit for finding Bailey today but gave credit where it was due. There aren't many men on the force that would do that."

Again, silence fell over the room. Avery was starting to wonder if they were looking for an apology out of her. If that were the case, they were going to be sorely disappointed.

Instead, O'Malley said something that floored her—something she had not been expecting.

"When this one is all over, and the last of the paperwork is filed away and Phillip Bailey is behind bars, we want to talk to you about a promotion to sergeant."

She was speechless. Words literally would not form on her tongue. *Did I hear him right?*

"Black?" Connelly asked.

"Thank you," she said. "But…I guess I just don't understand."

"You deserve it," Connelly said.

"More than that, I think you'd be a great sergeant," O'Malley said. "If you can bring the same results you produce as a detective to the position, it could be a great fit."

"Can I think about it?" Avery asked, still astounded.

"Yes," O'Malley said. "Think it over. We'll start the actual discussion on this when Bailey's case is done."

"And it is just about done," Connelly said. "Do you understand that, Black? This is our guy. Unless someone comes to the front door of the A1 with a confession that says otherwise, Phillip Bailey is our killer. So don't go digging this hole any deeper."

But what if we need to go deeper?

It was an alluring thought but she kept it to herself. In the wake of the totally unexpected conversation they had just had, it seemed foolish to stir up the hornet's nest.

"Again," O'Malley said, "good work today, you two. Now both of you go home and get some sleep."

With this comment made, Avery saw a thin smile touch the corners of Connelly's mouth. *He definitely suspects there's something going on with me and Ramirez,* she thought. *So much for keeping it a secret.*

O'Malley and Connelly left the room, closing the door behind them. Ramirez gave her a grin from across the table and shrugged. "Going home to get some sleep," he said. "Sounds like a pretty good idea, huh?"

"Maybe."

"We could go together," he said. "Maybe end up in the same bed."

"I don't think there would be much sleeping involved if we did that," Avery said.

Ramirez nodded, as if she had just made a very good point. "Still…I guess it doesn't matter," he said. "I've seen this look on your face before. You're not sure Bailey is the guy, are you?"

"There are some lingering doubts, yes."

"So you're working a late night, huh?"

She nodded. "Ramirez…the other night was great. It was better than great, actually. But I can't let that define our working relationship, too. And right now, until this case is really over, I don't know that I'd be able to draw a line between the two."

"I got it," he said. "You do your thing, Black. I'm going back to my little corner of the building and see what I can do to help wrap up the paperwork on this. If you need me, let me know."

She got the clear impression that this was his way of giving her a second chance—to come back home with him when she was done for the night.

"I will," she said. "Thanks, Ramirez."

He got up from his chair and gave her a light and reassuring squeeze on the shoulder as he passed her and made his exit. Avery was left alone at the table. She stared into space, feeling the sense of uncertainty wash over her.

If Bailey was not their guy, the killer was still out there. And if he had showed them anything so far, it was that he moved quickly—almost as quickly as the fire he used to kill his victims.

CHAPTER TWENTY SEVEN

He stared out of the passenger side window of the car, looking at the two-story house beside him. It was a nice house, complete with a pool in the backyard. The neighborhood wasn't a particularly nice one, but this woman lived on the nicer cul-de-sac. It was easily one of the nicest houses in the subdivision.

He had never met the woman but knew a good deal about her. Her name was Sophia Lesbrook. She was able to live in the house because her husband had worked as a very successful real estate broker. Her husband, though, had died two months ago. He had been able to get her address by calling the flower shop that had taken the bulk of orders from family and friends when her husband had passed away and placing his own fake order which he later cancelled.

Sophia had been a tough one to get. With the others, he had studied their movements and schedules. But Sophia had not gotten out much after her husband had died. She was fifty-two years old. They had never had any kids so she was living in this nice house by herself, visited only by a sister that stopped by once or twice a week. He knew this because this was not the first time he had parked across from her house. In fact, he'd done it six different times.

He was going to have to take some risks tonight if he wanted to procure her. He was pretty sure there were no electrical alarms or security systems within the house. He also knew where the spare key was; he had seen the sister take it from beneath one of the six flower pots that lined the porch.

He'd never broken into anyone's home before. In fact, up until he had taken Keisha Lawrence, he had never broken the law. He had done some things that he knew others would frown upon and might be considered deranged, but he had never broken the law.

So when he stepped out of his car and headed for Sophia Lesbrook's house, there was a whole new excitement to it. He had no gun, he had no knife…but he did have the drive behind his work and a pair of hands with the full strength of his toned arms behind them.

It was two in the morning and the entire subdivision was eerily quiet. It made every movement he made seem thunderously loud. He made his way up onto the porch and quietly lifted the fourth flower pot from the right. The silver spare key glittered in the moonlight like a beacon.

He picked it up and the feel of it sent a shock of excitement through him. He was really going to do this. He was about to cross a line that could never be uncrossed. Now it was more than just the fire that drove him...now it was the sense that he could do anything he wanted and could not be stopped.

He slid the key into the front door lock. When he turned it, his mind oddly turned to thoughts of his mother. She would be so disappointed in him. Breaking and entering. Kidnapping. Murder. He had clearly not become the upright young man she had desired him to be.

Well, fuck her, he thought. *This is her fault. She did this to me. She sent me on this path.*

It felt like a thin excuse but it was good enough for him.

After his father had died, his mother had kept his ashes in an urn on the mantel in the living room. He had been twelve when it happened, staring at that urn for more than seven years until he finally moved out. He recalled the arguments his mother and grandmother had often had. His grandmother tearing into his mother because she claimed her son had not wanted to be cremated. It had been nowhere in his will and he had deserved to be buried in the family plot out by their church. But his mother had always insisted that it had been the right thing to do. He would stare at that urn sometimes and wonder how someone's entire life and being could be held by it.

When he was twenty, his mother had made him spread the ashes. They'd done it out at a lake where no one had been in attendance. She had been drunk as he scattered the ashes, murmuring about how this was what he would have wanted...this was the best thing. By that point, his grandmother had moved to another state and there had been no arguments. And he had felt that it had been very wrong.

It had seemed wrong to him then and it still seemed wrong. To burn someone's dead body when they had not wanted such a thing for their final remains. To scatter them in what had seemed like a random location was even worse. He'd hated his mother for it for the longest time. It made him think of her as a witch who had kept his ashes for emotional reasons he had never quite understood.

When he opened the door to Sophia Lesbrook's house, he almost hoped his mother was hearing it wherever she was these days. He hoped she was dreaming it and that this act of disobedience was pulling her from her sleep.

Ahead of him, the house was dreary and dark. It was a lovely house, the living room opening up on the right to show a fifty-inch

121

television over a fireplace set into the wall. Everything was immaculately cleaned and he could smell something that had been baking earlier in the day—cinnamon rolls, perhaps.

He ventured through the house, enjoying the thrill of seeing the interior of a house he did not belong in. But he did not let himself get distracted. He went from room to room, finally finding Sophia's bedroom upstairs.

She slept with a noise machine on the bedside table. It was tuned to basic white noise, a hiss that made the room feel small in an odd way.

He stepped to the side of the bed and watched her sleep for a few seconds. With a slight frown, he then made a fist of his right hand, drew it back, and delivered a hard punch to the side of her head.

Her eyes sprang open as she sprang hard to the right. She opened her mouth to cry out but his hand was quick to cover her lips. He crawled onto the bed and straddled her. He drew his right hand back and hit her again. This time, an ache went spiraling through his wrist. Beneath him, her body went limp.

In an almost anticlimactic way, he removed himself from the bed and looked down at her. He removed the covers from her body and stared at her. She was pretty for her age and he wondered what it might be like to be the kind of man that would take advantage of her unconscious body. But that was not him. He would never sink to those depraved depths.

But really…he had never thought he'd break into someone's house. How much further was he capable of going?

With some effort, he was able to get her out of the bed. He carried her threshold style, feeling the slight rise and fall of her breaths against him. He carried her down the stairs and looked back into the living room. He paused for a moment before leaving.

He stared into the living room. On the mantel between the fireplace and the television, there were a few pictures of family members and of a man he assumed had been Sophia's husband.

And in the midst of it all, there was an urn…the final resting place of her husband's ashes until they were scattered.

But with her gone, he didn't think those ashes would ever be scattered.

He gave the urn a final longing look and then carried Sophia's unconscious body back out into the night.

CHAPTER TWENTY EIGHT

Avery gave up on the hope of sleep sometime after one in the morning. She put on a fresh pot of coffee in the A1 break room and was on her second cup when her thoughts once again turned to her odd meeting with Howard Randall. Randall had never been one to just hand out information. He preferred to provide clues in an almost cryptic form, making her work for it.

Is that what he was doing when I visited him? she wondered. *Was his mood a hint?*

It was a stretch. All she knew was that his insistence that she never visit him again was not like him at all. He usually enjoyed her visits, mainly because he got off on the fact that someone of her caliber relied on his insights. So why the sudden the change of a heart?

It made her wonder if his direction had been misleading. He had suggested that she not worry so much about the arson aspect of fire...that it was totally symbolic. She agreed with it but it was hard to find a suspect based on nothing more than symbolism. There had to be something else...something she was missing.

She rifled through the papers on her desk and pulled out the details on the victims. She read through them a few times, waiting for a link to jump out at her.

All women so far.

The third was rushed, the body not burned. No positive ID as of yet.

The manner in which he leaves the remains indicates that he wants our attention but has no desire to be caught. He wants to gloat about what he's doing but is content to do it for the attention.

That again made her think of what she and Dr. Sloane Miller had discussed. Arsonists often revisited the scene of their crime to *watch* the destruction. So maybe the killer was coming back to his crime scenes to watch Avery and her fellow detectives and law enforcement officials try to figure out the method to his madness. But why? What was it about their psychological makeup that drove them to do such a thing?

There was another question, still: if he was using fire as a symbolic means, maybe the symbolism didn't stop at the fire. Maybe it came down to the victims, too.

What am I missing?

She was about to pore over the information on the victims again when a knock sounded out at her already open door. She looked up and saw Ramirez peeking in. He looked tired but still had that boyish sort of energy to him when he smiled at her.

"Anything new?" he asked.

"No. Just dead ends and frustration. You?"

"Phillip Bailey has a lawyer coming in tomorrow morning. He'd still insisting he has never killed a person—that his perversions never extended beyond animals."

"So things with him are at a stand-still for now?" she asked.

"Yeah, until tomorrow when the lawyer comes in. Why? You still have your doubts?"

"I do, but I don't know why."

"Well, give your brain a rest," he said. He walked into the office and walked behind her as she remained sitting. He started to massage her shoulders and she instantly felt herself relax. She couldn't remember the last time a man had rubbed her back.

"My brain never rests," she said. "And Ramirez…while what you're doing feels amazing, that's crossing the line we keep talking about."

"To hell with that line. There's no one else on this floor right now."

"We still have work to do," she said. She was starting to get irritated. How many different ways did she have to tell him that she did not want their romantic entanglements to interfere with their work? She really didn't want to be a bitch about it, but he was leaving her no choice.

"You work your ass off," Ramirez said. "It's okay to take five or ten minutes for yourself." As he said this, he increased the pressure on his shoulders. His hands also slid a bit lower below her neck.

"For what?" she asked, shrugging off his hands. "You want me to just throw everything on my desk onto the floor so you can bang me on it? Want a quickie on my desk? Or maybe in a janitor's closet? Jesus, Ramirez…grow up and do your job."

"No, I didn't want a quickie on your desk," he said, offended.

"Then what is it?" she asked. "What *do* you want?"

"Ten minutes with you where we aren't bogged down by our jobs," he said.

"Well, you aren't going to get that right now. I'm sorry, but if you make me choose between work and you, you're not going to stand much of a chance."

"Oh," he said, slowly walking back to the door. "It's that easy for you, huh?"

"Yes. It is."

"So maybe I should just leave you alone until this case is wrapped...or until you decide that you're overthinking it and it's already wrapped. Bailey is our guy. Stop overthinking things. Stop *making* yourself busy so you can ignore this emotional thing you're feeling for me."

"That's *not* what I'm doing," she spat.

"I'm not too sure about that," Ramirez said.

"The world does not revolve around you," Avery said. "Now, if you don't mind...close the door on your way out."

It was obvious that he was biting back a remark as he made his exit, but he managed to swallow it down. He *did* put some force behind closing the door as he left, though.

Avery looked back down to the files of the victims. All women...but what else? Was there something there that she was missing?

She thought of her conversation with Sloane and the insights she had given into the mind of an arsonist. Maybe they needed to look at it from a different angle—from a fresh perspective. Of course, it was nearing three in the morning right now so there was very little to be done.

Knowing that three hours of sleep would be useless, she stood up and stretched her back. She then settled back down behind the desk and studied the files for Keisha Lawrence and Sarah Osborne. She hoped the identity of the third victim might help tie up some loose ends.

But until then, she only had the two deceased women staring at her from pieces of paper on her desk. They had been reduced to ashes on their last days on earth and it was up to Avery to discover the stories they had to tell.

She thought of Dr. Sloane Miller again and thought she might be just the person to help her figure out what these particularly tragic stories meant.

CHAPTER TWENTY NINE

Avery waited until six in the morning to call Sloane. She was relieved to hear that it sounded like Sloane had been awake for quite some time already. As it so happened, she was in a coffee shop when she answered her phone and happily agreed to meet with Avery the moment she got to the office.

That's how Avery came to be sitting in Sloane's office half an hour later with a coffee and a muffin Sloane had brought her from the coffee shop. Sloane set her things down on her desk, powered up her work laptop, and finally took a seat.

"So what can I do for you?" Sloane asked.

"I'm still hung up on this case where the killer is burning his victims," Avery said. She was sitting in the patient's chair, eating her small breakfast. For a moment, it almost felt as if she were just hanging out with a close friend. "I'm trying to view it through the lens of someone who might be using fire as a strictly symbolic means without any interest or leaning towards arson."

"Well, that's certainly interesting," Sloane said. "But I'm not sure you'll find someone fitting that description. I guess it *is* possible, but unlikely."

"And why do you say that?"

Sloane thought about it for a moment as she sipped from her coffee. "As we discussed before, even a little kid staring into a campfire—maybe holding a hot dog or marshmallow over it—understands the power that fire has. There's an inherent sort of respect for it. What an arsonist essentially does is evolve that fascination and respect into a device for power. They want to see the world burn and they have no problem using fire to do it because it's an outlet of power to them. Does that make sense?"

"So far, yes," Avery said.

"So now let's consider someone who is burning bodies on purpose. Sure, there could be some symbolism attached to it and that's fine. But anyone using fire as a means to destroy or reduce something is working on those same inherent feelings. They understand the absolute power of fire and are using it with intent. It may even be a situation where the killer doesn't even realize he has these arson-like tendencies. But at the root of what he's doing, there is a degree of the same sort of mindset an arsonist would have, even if it's at its most basic form."

So it could be someone like Phillip Bailey, Avery thought. *Behind his obvious mental issues, there's an almost primitive understanding of how fire is a very basic yet common way to destroy things. Hell, even George Lutz understood that.*

"So you think it would be a mistake to rule out an arsonist?" Avery asked.

"I wouldn't do it. In fact, I'd be looking for links between the two. Out of your suspects, is there anyone who has a background in arson that also may have some sort of connection to fire that could be viewed as symbolic?"

Would an arsonist work at a crematorium or trash-burning plant? Avery wondered. *And if they did, would they even understand why they were doing it? Would they even be aware of their interest in fire?*

Avery nodded, knowing exactly what she needed to look for. But on the heels of that was the question of Howard Randall. Had he purposefully given her wrong information? Had he just been screwing with her, tiring of being her lackluster mentor?

Symbolism versus intent, Avery thought. *I've been putting too much stake in that thought. What if the two are married? What if we're looking for someone who is not only very much aware of their obsession with fire, but with the mindset of a killer?*

There's no need to look at those as individual traits if they could be linked to create a sadistic murderer.

But then again, maybe Howard was right all along. Maybe the killer was using fire as a weapon but not with an arsonist's frame of mind. Sometimes, fire was just fire.

"Does that help?" Sloane asked.

"I think it does. And as much as I hate to take the gift of coffee and run..."

"Run," Sloane said with a smile of understanding. "Go get the bad guy, Detective Black."

With a nod of appreciation, Avery left Sloane's office with the cogs in her head already turning. She walked back to her own office on autopilot as she started putting the pieces together in her head.

By the time she was back behind her desk, she was pretty sure she knew exactly what she was looking for—and that two files in particular were on her desk that lined up almost exactly.

In their searches, Avery had received files based on people with a history of arson and then a completely different set of files based on people who had worked at crematoriums and had been let go for questionable reasons. While she had done *some* cross-referencing, she had not done anything in-depth because she had been leaning so hard toward arson not being a part of it.

She pulled up the two files that had shown the most promise when she had been cross-referencing the material. The first one was an older woman who had worked in a crematorium between 1989 and 2006. She had not been fired but had quit because of health concerns. She had come back for a few years to work as a receptionist before retiring for good in 2012. There was a mark of arson on her record, but it came from 1986 when she had been arrested for possession of marijuana and opiates. The arson in question was speculated to be perhaps an accidental fire started in her friend's backyard that had nearly burned the house down.

The second file was much more interesting, though. It told the story of a man named Roosevelt Toms. He had been employed by Everett Brothers Crematorium between 2006 and 2012. He had been fired for what the file listed as "professional difference of opinion from that of the owners." Avery looked back through the other pile and did not find his name to cross-reference. However, in his file within the crematorium employees, there was an additional sheet of information attached. It was a brief document that explained that Roosevelt had been arrested in 2001 under an intent-to-harm charge. Later that year, a girlfriend had called the police on him due to suicidal tendencies when he locked himself in the attic of their apartment.

Near the end of the report, a small statement caught Avery's attention and made her stand up from the desk.

When he locked himself in the attic, Roosevelt carried two things with him: a lighter and a small can of gasoline from beneath the patio where the lawnmower was kept.

Bingo, Avery thought.

She gathered up the files and thumbed in the number for Everett Brothers Crematorium. She was out her door and headed down the hallways toward the parking garage before the phone had even started ringing.

CHAPTER THIRTY

Avery could see right away that Charles Everett was uneasy with a detective stepping into his place of business. Avery didn't quite understand this, as it was a beautiful building that didn't have that morbid sort of feel that had saturated Wallace Funeral Home. She tried to remind herself that it was only 8:40 in the morning when she stepped into his office and that this was probably not the way he wanted to start his day.

"Thanks for meeting with me on short notice," Avery said.

"It's not a problem," he said. "But I have to admit...I was hoping I'd go the rest of my life without hearing the name of Roosevelt Toms. Everyone around here always called him Rosie for short...something he hated and I found sort of off-putting. Because there was nothing rosy about him."

"Can you tell me a little bit about him?"

"Well, my brother hired him and he's been deceased for five years now, God rest his soul. But I originally saw some of the same things in Rosie that he did. He was a hard worker and seemed to genuinely care about the bodies that came through here. Also, if we were in a pinch and needed someone to work the floor during memorial services, he was great at consoling people. But if I'm being honest...there was always something about him that never sat right with me. He was one of those people that just sort of started to creep you out after you spent a lot of time with him."

"How so?" Avery asked.

"I don't know, exactly. He'd sometimes have this blank stare, like he was thinking really hard about something that he didn't want you to know about. And there were times when I'd catch him just staring at the deceased...not in a sad way but...I don't know. It was almost the same way a curious middle school kid would look at a toad just before they put it on the dissection tray. You know what I mean?"

Or like a cat in Phillip Bailey's basement, Avery thought. It was a little alarming how these sorts of people were starting to link themselves together in her head.

"And why was he fired?" Avery asked. "The only explanation I have is *professional difference of opinion from that of the owners.*"

"It was the strangest thing...whenever he got the chance, he'd actively try to talk our clients out of cremation. He told them burial was a more natural way to respect the bodies. He was very passionate about it."

That's a new avenue to consider, she thought. *Someone using fire as more than a weapon, but almost like a spiteful punishment—someone who* doesn't *necessarily like fire.*

"Any idea why he started doing this?" Avery asked.

"No idea. But it got annoying. He'd even start lecturing us about it. And one day it was just too much. We let him go."

"And did he get hostile about your decision to fire him?"

"Not at all," Charles said. "In fact, it was all rather civil. He even called and apologized several months later."

"But you said there was nothing *rosy* about him," Avery said.

"I did. Even in that phone call where he tried apologizing, he had this way of just getting under your skin. His voice was flat and monotone. And it seemed like an act—like he was hiding something from us and was taking a great deal of pleasure from it."

Maybe he wanted back in, Avery thought. *Maybe something about fire drew him back...maybe he realized this sort of workplace could greatly benefit whatever skewed plans he was forming.*

"Mr. Everett, do you know where I might be able to find Roosevelt Toms? We have no current residence on file."

"The last address I have for him is the apartment he used to live in. But I know for a fact he moved out of that shortly before he was fired from here."

Avery thought about the information in the file. She thought about the man Charles Everett had just described to her, climbing into the attic with a lighter and gasoline. That scene, coupled with what she had just learned about him, made her think that she might finally be on the right trail.

"What about next of kin or emergency contacts?" Avery asked.

"Yes, I can get those for you but keep in mind, they're going to be at least four years old."

"That will be fine for a start. Thanks, Mr. Everett."

"Of course," he said as he started tapping at keys on his laptop. He worked quickly, giving Avery casual glances as he worked. It took him less than thirty seconds to get the information he needed. When it was on his screen, he printed a copy out on an old printer that hummed on a shelf behind the desk. He grabbed the single sheet of paper and handed it to Avery.

"Here you go," he said. "I hope it helps." He paused for a moment with a thoughtful look on his face and asked:"Can I ask you something, Detective?"

"Of course."

130

"I saw something on the news last night…a story about a killer that seemed to be burning his victims, some to the point of near cremation. Is Rosie being eyed in this?"

"I'm afraid I can't discuss case details with you," Avery said.

"Ah, I understand," Charles said. But there was an understanding in his eyes, letting her know that the template answer she had given had, in fact, answered his question. "Best of luck to you on the case."

"Thanks."

She excused herself from the office, holding the paper tightly. As she exited Everett Brothers Crematorium, she didn't realize how suffocated she had felt until she was back out in the fresh air. Even though the place had been airy, clean, and mostly cheerful, Avery hoped she would never have to step foot into another funeral home or crematorium until it was her own body lying on the slab.

CHAPTER THIRTY ONE

The address Avery had been given was for a woman named Debbie Toms, listed as *mother* on the emergency contacts form Charles Everett had given her. The house was in a middle-class part of town. The front was surrounded with modest flower beds, and a small birdbath sat in the side yard.

Avery knocked on the door for five minutes and got no answer. She had no solid ages to do math with but figured there was a good chance that Debbie had not yet retired and was working a job. She made the call to A1 for assistance and was asked to hold while the receptionist transferred the call.

She was beyond surprised when Ramirez answered the page. When she heard his voice, she froze for a moment, unsure of how to proceed.

"Hey," she finally said.

"Hey yourself," he said. "What do you need?"

He was quick and to the point. It was quite clear that he had no interest in speaking to her beyond the formalities of the job.

"I need some information on a woman named Debbie Toms, particularly her current place of employment."

"Is this for the firebug case?"

She sighed, not wanting to get into it with him. She reminded herself that as far as Ramirez, O'Malley, and Connelly were concerned, Phillip Bailey was the guilty party and they currently had him in custody.

"Can you just get someone on that for me, please?" Avery asked.

"Will do. I'll get someone to call you with it as soon as possible."

"Thanks," she said, but the line was dead before the word was out of her mouth.

Well, if I hadn't pissed him off enough before to scare him away, I sure as hell did a great job of it last night.

She went back to her car and looked over the material on Roosevelt "Rosie" Toms again. She knew there was nothing of real use there, but she wanted to drill the information into her head.

As she read over it, her phone rang. Again, she was surprised to hear Ramirez on the other end. She'd been sure he would have tasked someone else with the menial job of finding someone's current employer.

"I've got that information for you," Ramirez said without any sort of greeting. "Debbie Toms works as a packager for a Dollar General distribution center. Looks like a shift-work sort of deal."

"Can you shoot me the address?"

"Yeah. And look…the reason I called you back…I'm going to ask O'Malley to assign me to something else today. Agent Duggan is out of the picture now because he's convinced Bailey is the guilty party, too. So I'm solo again. I'm not going to tell O'Malley what you're off doing right now because it might piss him off. There's a possible kidnapping that was reported this morning. I might see if I can get some action on that."

"A kidnapping?" Avery asked.

"Well, not a *kid*. Some woman went missing. Sophia Lesbrook. It's an interesting one because her husband died a few months ago. There's some speculation that his death might be connected to her being taken."

"Well, good luck on it. Let me know if you need any h—"

"What?" he asked.

It's a long shot, Avery thought even before she replied. Still, it was worth checking out. "Do we know how her husband died?"

"Car accident. He hung on in the hospital for a few hours but it was a lost cause from the start from what I hear. Why?"

"Where was he buried?" she asked.

"What kind of question is that?"

"Can you just answer it?"

"Hold on," he said bitterly. "Hold on. I've got the files right here. Um…well, he wasn't buried. He was cremated and…oh, Avery. That's a stretch. That's more than a stretch. That's more like a *bend*."

"Can you do some digging for me?" she asked.

He sighed but it might as well have been a *yes*. "What kind of digging?"

"Look into Keisha Lawrence and Sarah Osborne. See if they had any loved ones pass away over the last year or so. And if there were deaths, see if they were buried or cremated."

"Are you serious?" he asked. But even in that question, she knew she had him hooked. She could hear the edge of excitement in his voice.

"Yes, I am. Can you do that for me?"

Again, another heavy sigh came from his end. "I'll get back to you as soon as I get the results."

"Thanks, Ramirez."

"Uh-huh."

The line went dead and Avery supposed that an *uh-huh* was much better than a cold disconnection like the last time. Within a few seconds, as promised, he texted her the address to the distribution center Debbie Toms worked at. It was almost like he was right there by her side, helping her out again.

With things slowly starting to fall into place like a morbid puzzle in her head, Avery plugged the address into her GPS. Finally, she felt like she was getting somewhere. She was so certain that it took everything within her not to cut the flashers and sirens on to race across town to find out if her hunches would pay off.

***

The distribution center was an enormous maze of a place. Without the receptionist to lead her through the stacks and stacks of merchandise being shipped out, Avery would have never been able to find Debbie Toms. As it happened, Debbie was working along one of the conveyor belts that sent the merchandise to several other belts to then be sorted into the delivery trucks. The receptionist had a word with the shift supervisor and the supervisor then led Avery to a woman at the far end of the belt.

Debbie Tom was a small woman who probably looked older than she really was. There was a slight slump to her posture and her face looked as if the muscles around her mouth had been frozen into a permanent scowl.

The supervisor gestured toward Debbie as if to say *she's all yours now* and then went back to his station. Avery approached her, almost feeling sad for the woman. Avery guessed her to be about sixty to sixty-five—and this was the type of job a woman of that age took mainly because there was very little retirement money waiting for her.

"My name is Detective Avery Black," Avery said. "I need to speak with you for a moment. Your supervisor has offered his office."

Debbie Toms said nothing at first. She just looked down to where her supervisor was still walking to the other end of the belt and rolled her eyes. "Okay," she said finally. "But can I ask what this is about?"

"I'm with the Homicide Division, Boston PD. We're neck-deep in a case that has raised the name of your son."

Again, Debbie gave a roll of the eyes. "Fuckin' Roosevelt," she said. "Come on, let's get to it, then."

They were in the small and rather smelly office of the shift supervisor three minutes later. Neither of them sat, although Debbie's back seemed to scream for some sort of a break.

"You didn't seem surprised that I mentioned your son," Avery said.

"Not really," Debbie said. "He's never been in any real trouble that I know of. But he's the kind that's like a bomb. You know, one day he's just going to go off. I've felt that about him since he was sixteen and got into his first fight at school. Of course, I haven't spoken to him in nearly five years, so what the hell do I know?"

"Did he ever do any jail time that you know of?"

"He spent two nights in jail when he was twenty-five or so for drunk and disorderly behavior. And there was one time when the cops were looking into him for some arson-related crimes. But no…nothing serious."

Arson, she thought. *It keeps popping up. Maybe there's a reason I can't seem to get away from it as a lead.*

"If you don't mind my asking, why has it been so long since you spoke?"

"He got involved with some girl that broke his heart," Debbie said. "Most boys come back home after that, you know? But Roosevelt was the opposite. He did some traveling…mostly within the States. When he came back around here and settled down, he wanted nothing to do with me. And as a mother, I hate to say this…but I didn't really care. He had changed somehow. He was *darker* if that makes sense."

"We've got some things on record about him being possibly involved with arson, like you mentioned. Do you recall him having any sort of obsession with fire when he was younger?"

"Not that I can recall. He used to burn things in the backyard. G.I. Joes, He-Man figures, little Matchbox cars, things like that. But I figured it was normal for a boy of his age."

That might be the first steps toward burning animals in coolers, Avery thought. *And maybe even human bodies in some sort of hidden firebox.*

"Do you happen to know where he's living now?" Avery asked.

"No clue. I know he had a job around here for a while at some crematorium. He was living in a rundown apartment back then. But I haven't heard from him since then. I ran into an old friend of his a few months back that said they were pretty sure he was living in Texas somewhere."

"I see," Avery said, slowly starting to feel this lead crumble away. She was just about to ask another question, anything that might link Roosevelt Toms back to the Boston area, when her phone rang. She glanced at the display and saw that it was Ramirez. "Sorry," she said to Debbie. "I need to take this. It'll just take a second."

Debbie nodded slowly, as if she couldn't care less. Avery stepped out of the office and put her finger into her ear to filter the noise of the machinery in the factory.

"I'm glad you called," Avery said in lieu of *hello.* "I need you to do every kind of search you can on a Roosevelt Toms. There's a good chance he's living in Texas and has a spotty record."

"Yeah, I can do that," Ramirez said. "But while I'm doing that, let me give you some news to soak in."

His tone was rather excited. Either he was managing to put the remarks of the previous night behind him or he had come across something that had changed his attitude.

"What did you find?" Avery asked.

"For starters, the identity of the third victim. Her name was Mary Sawyer, forty-one years of age."

"Any family to notify?"

"That's where it gets good," Ramirez said. "Damn it, Avery…you were right. We went back and looked deep into the other victims. Keisha Lawrence lost her mother about five months ago to breast cancer. They were a small family and Keisha had been put in charge of final arrangements. Her mother was cremated and her ashes were spread somewhere on a beach in North Carolina.

"Then there's Sarah Osborne. She's a real strange one. She was too young to have to make the decision to cremate someone. But when her golden retriever died earlier this year, she cremated it. According to what we know, Fido's ashes are still in a little urn somewhere in a stack of boxes that was taken from her apartment after she died."

"My God," Avery said. "And how about this new woman, Mary Sawyer?"

"A brother…died of heart failure at fifty-two years of age. He was cremated nine weeks ago."

"And the missing woman you were talking about, Sophia Lesbrook," Avery said. "Her husband was cremated."

"Yeah, we're working on the assumption that it can't be a coincidence. We're assembling a team to comb her house right now."

"Sounds good. In the meantime, please see what you can do to pull some information on Roosevelt Toms—maybe under the nickname of Rosie. If he's in Texas, he's an eliminated lead. But if there's any doubt of his location, I think he might be our guy."

"And if Mary Sawyer is indeed the next victim," Ramirez said, "that shows that Phillip Bailey is innocent because he's been in our custody for the last twelve hours."

"And most importantly," Avery said, "it proves that the killer is still out there."

CHAPTER THIRTY TWO

Sophia Lesbrook came to slowly. It was almost like waking up from a very bad dream, only there was pain to go along with the fear. It was a pain that started along the right side of her jaw and seem to trace its way halfway down her back. She tasted blood in her mouth and something about the inside of her mouth felt weird. She lolled her head to the right very slowly and realized the lower half of the right side of her face was badly swollen.

That's when she remembered the fleeting image of the man in her bedroom. She had no idea where he had come from and by the time she'd been aware that he was in bed with her and straddling her, it had been too late.

She opened her eyes quickly, an action that seemed to cause the pain in her face and back to intensify.

She was in a room that looked sort of like a basement. She was lying on a cold concrete floor. There was light in the room but it was faint. She saw through her hazy vision that it was coming from a small lamp that sat on a table across the room. A man was sitting at the table, his back to her. He seemed to be concentrating hard on something but she could not see what it was.

She wanted to scream but fought the urge. She did her best to take a quick inventory of her body. Her face hurt like hell and with each second she regained her consciousness, she started to realize that the pain that spiraled down her back seemed to also radiate at the base along the back of her neck.

The taste of blood in her mouth was thick but she didn't think there was any actively coming out of her mouth. Looking back to the image of the man in her bed, she instantly wondered if she had been raped but she didn't seem to be harmed in that way. Sure, he could have done a lot of things that would leave no pain or traces of foul play but for now, the fair certainty that she had not been raped was good enough for her.

Then what does he want?

It was a good question. And it was not one she could get an answer to at the moment. His back was still to her and she could still not tell what he was looking at. What she *was* aware of, though, was that he had started muttering to himself. It was a high-pitched and urgent sort of voice that made her wonder if he might be mentally challenged.

She then eyed the room she was in. Her head was resting in the far corner, giving her a decent view of the room. A few feet away from her head there was a rather large door. There was a strange-looking lock on the outside of it and the U-shaped handle reminded her of the walk-in freezer at the butcher shop her grandfather had once owned.

On the other end of the room, there was a standard door. It was closed most of the way but not completely. In the murkiness on the other side, she could see the beginning of a set of wooden stairs.

The idea of running for her life crossed her mind. His back was to her and he was preoccupied. As if to prove this farther, he continued muttering to himself. This time, she caught a few of the words.

"...too damn hard...and now you killed the bitch...still burn but so what...?"

He thinks I'm dead, Sophia thought. *I really could get the jump on him. If I move my ass right now, I could make it to those stairs before he got out of his chair.*

But she also knew that beyond those stairs, she'd be unfamiliar with the building above them. All it would take was one wrong turn and he'd have her. And then maybe he *would* kill her...and on purpose this time.

Best to play dead for now, Sophia thought. *I'll play dead until I get a better idea of what he's up to...or when I know I can get a good head start on him.*

Suddenly, he was turning in his chair. He turned toward her and she closed her eyes. She opened them the tiniest bit, into something thinner than slits. She could barely see him or the object he was holding in his hand. She was pretty sure it was something almost like a large can, something that had a dull shine to it in the lamplight from the desk.

He was looking at her, perhaps studying her. Hadn't he said something about burning? Was he sizing her up for something?

She didn't know. She concentrated on taking extremely shallow breaths, ready to hold in completely if he came over to her for a closer evaluation.

But he did not do that. He turned back around and placed the object he had been holding on the side of the desk. He started to study something else, setting something out on the desk with loving care. As she watched him, he pulled small box from under the desk. He piled more of it onto the desk. It was odd...but Sophia was pretty sure it was foam or some sort of insulation carpenters used before putting up drywall or sheetrock. She also saw a small container on the edge of the desk. It was yellow with a red top.

Is that lighter fluid?

139

The insulation and the lighter fluid were weird, sure…but when she was able to finally see the object he had placed on the desk, her heart sank and she felt the need to scream again.

It was an urn.

And she was pretty sure the man had not been talking to himself the entire time. Sophia was pretty sure he had been talking to the urn.

Oh my God, he's insane.

She started to tremble and even felt a scream rising up in her throat. If she let out as much as a tiny moan, he'd know she was alive and then…well, she didn't know what would happen.

So she closed her eyes and played dead, the darkness behind her eyes much more favorable than his weird actions. But as hard as she tried, she could not help herself; she had to open her eyes a bit to see what was going on.

Time and time again, her eyes were drawn back to that golden urn sitting on the edge of the desk. Having heard the man speak of burning while holding an urn was bad enough. But having an almost supernatural certainty of what was inside the urn was what truly made Sarah's heart thunder and her mind tremble with the certainty that she would not be *pretending* to be dead much longer.

CHAPTER THIRTY THREE

When Avery arrived back at the A1, the conference room and just about every office in Homicide was alive with a flurry of activity. People who had looked confident and almost bored the day before were now bouncing from the walls with excitement and energy. The moment Connelly spotted her hurrying toward her own office, he cut her off in the hallway.

"See," he said with a smirk. "It's things like *this* that make you both very frustrating to work with and a prime candidate for a sergeant position. There's so much excitement around here that O'Malley isn't even all that mad at you for going against his orders *again*."

"So where are we?" she asked.

"I'm not so sure myself. We keep getting reports coming in on both avenues—the victims having cremated loved ones in the recent past as well as possible locations for a Roosevelt Toms. We've even got a few FBI analysts helping remotely. Duggan is also back in the A1. The FBI really is being generous with this one…handing us resources without trying to take it away from us…*yet*."

They walked as they talked, making it to the conference room where they both knew O'Malley would be doing his best to rein things in. When they entered, she saw that O'Malley was scribbling something on the room's whiteboard. One of the data guys was tapping something into a laptop while Finley was busy trying to connect a Skype call through his laptop and onto the projector screen on the wall opposite the white board. She also spotted Ramirez as she found a seat at the table. He gave her a nod of acknowledgment and nothing more.

Avery caught bits and pieces of conversations here and there and they all seemed to wrap up with the same point: there were still no definitive answers. The one thing she *did* hear that was on the positive side of things was that Phillip Bailey had been released to a psychiatric doctor and he was no longer being considered a suspect.

When the room was crammed with about fifteen people, O'Malley cleared his throat and yelled for order. He then looked to Officer Finley and asked: "We good?"

"Yes, sir. We're up."

With that, Finley projected a Skype window onto the screen on the far wall. A man Avery had never seen was on the screen, looking just as excited as everyone in the room with her.

"You're on, Agent Lewis," Finley said.

"Okay," Lewis said. "I'm Agent Don Lewis with the FBI out of the Boston office. I'm leading up the data and analysis team, trying to find Roosevelt Toms. We've got five other agents on this and so far, after about two hours, we have nothing. We have a ton of dead ends, but there is no definitive address to be found on record. It's almost like the man disappeared."

"And how is that possible?" O'Malley asked from the head of the conference table.

"Well, he could be dead, for one. I know that leads your team to a dead end but it's an avenue we have to consider. There's also the chance that he's now living under an alias. Given his past record, I think that might be a safe bet. And if that's the case we can still track him down, but it would be tricky as hell. We do have one picture of him—it's about five years old, but should do the trick."

Lewis flashed a color printout of what looked like a candid Facebook profile picture to the conference room. Avery stared at it, committing the face to memory. "From what we can tell, this was a picture provided years ago, taken candidly by someone he once worked with when he was being investigated."

"Rest assured," O'Malley said, "we've got a team of officers and detectives on this thing here, too. Anything you need from us, just let us know."

"We will," Lewis said. "The bureau is taking this case very seriously. If there's no arrest made within the next few hours I'd fully expect at least one more agent to show on the scene down there. I assume Agent Duggan has been of some value?"

"Some," O'Malley said, and left it at that.

"Yes...well...just let us know what we can do to help."

"Sounds good," O'Malley said. Avery smirked because she knew the last thing O'Malley would want was another FBI agent in the midst of things. "Thanks, Agent Lewis."

With that, Finley ended the call and all eyes were back on O'Malley. "Well, you heard the man," O'Malley said. "We're basically looking for a ghost when it comes to Roosevelt Toms. Beyond that, we can now confirm that the three cremations we were looking into from the victims' families were *not* done at the same crematorium, knocking out *that* possible link and motive."

"What about landlords or renters?" Avery asked.

"We've got details on two and they all give us an address in Texas that leads to a dead end," O'Malley said. "If Roosevelt Toms *is* out there, he covered his tracks well. I hate to say it, but at this point it a snipe hunt. We have to beat the streets, make calls that are going to probably come up with dead ends, and hope to get lucky. Black, do you have anything to add?"

She was aware that all eyes were on her. It was a feeling she did not mind at all but could not seem to get used to. There was respect in most of the faces that looked at her and maybe even a little bit of anxiousness and anticipation. It made her feel like the case hinged on what she chose to do next—and that was fine with her.

I guess it's my show now, she thought. *Maybe this is like some messed up test from O'Malley to see if he's right about wanting me for a sergeant position.*

"It might be a good idea to send some cars by the previous sites where the remains were found," Avery said. "If he's using fire as some symbolic device *and* has an arsonist's mentality, there's a good chance he might revisit the scene for some sick sort of motivation or nostalgia."

"I'll get two cars out on that right now," he said. "Anyone else?"

Silence around the table was the only answer. O'Malley waited less than two seconds before giving a thunderous clap of his hands. "That's it, then. Every single one of you will be notified when something new comes to us. For now, get out there and hunt this bastard down."

Everyone filed out of the room quickly, like they were in a fire drill. Avery noticed that Ramirez was hanging back, slowly making his way over to her. He did so confidently and she admired him for that. It seemed that he was remaining professional and trying to forget how she had treated him in terms of their romantic relationship. It had to take some serious fortitude on his part.

He came over to her and stood close. He held eye contact with her and she felt something tug at her heart. *I trust this man,* she thought. *I trust this man with my life and I'm pretty damn lucky that he wants anything to do with me outside of work.*

"Where do you need me on this?" he asked.

She wondered if this was his way of asking her if she needed him to be by her side. She nearly said exactly that but then put the job before her heart—the same thing that had caused her to lash out at him on two occasions in the last two days. But in this regard, she was pretty sure he appreciated it.

"Honestly, I don't even know. It's all research right now and I hate to waste your talents on that."

"Look. Put me where you need me. I'm fine with it."

143

"I wonder if we need to dig deeper into these three cremations. Maybe there's something else about the families that links them— not only to one another but to the killer."

"So you want me to talk to extended family members."

"I think it might be a good idea. It might even—"

"Detective Black?" someone said from behind her.

She turned and saw Agent Duggan coming quickly into the room through the last of the officers to file out. He was holding his phone in his hand and pointing it toward her.

"Agent Duggan," she said. "What is it?"

"I got this e-mail two minutes ago," he said. "It's a thin lead, but it's a lead. I had someone try to get in touch with the girlfriend that was living with Toms when he threatened suicide. That led to a dead end but it also led to the name and location of the man that lived with him as a roommate for six months. That roommate, by the way…arrested in 2009 on minor arson charges."

"Is he still local?" Avery asked.

"According to his electric and internet bills. But the weird thing is that he has some missing spaces in his history, too."

"That's fine; it's still a great lead. Can you shoot me over his information?"

"I can, but I thought it might be best if I just rode over with you."

Shit, she thought. But she managed an excuse fast, hoping he'd bite. She didn't have much experience with FBI agents but from what she had heard, they tended to get large egos when they were asked to work with those in the lower ranks.

"If it was more than just a six-month roommate, I'd agree," she said. "But I think I'm good with this. I'd rather you stay here just in case something hard-hitting comes in. It's your call, though."

Duggan considered this for a moment and then nodded. "Good call. I'll stay here. But I'd appreciate it if you call me if this turns into anything."

"Absolutely," Avery said, having no intention of doing any such thing.

"Good luck out there," Duggan said, looking back down to his phone. "I'm sending you the information right now."

"Thanks," she said.

He gave a nod and a wave before turning to leave the room. When he was gone, Ramirez smiled at her and shook his head. "You don't want some hotshot FBI agent riding around with you?" he asked.

"God no," she said.

144

"How about an overreaching partner-slash-lover?"

She was embarrassed that she felt herself trying not to blush. She reached out and took his hand, giving it a quick squeeze. "I actually think it's a good idea if you speak to the extended family. I'm not expecting much out of this visit. But when you're done, just give me a call. I'll forward you the information just in case you come up with nothing and have the time to join me."

"You sure?"

"Yeah," she said. "And listen...about everything I said the other night...hell, the last *two* nights..."

"Don't even go there," he said. "Not now, anyway. You were right last night. Business and pleasure need to be separated. I could explain to you why it's so difficult for me but it's small and unimportant compared to what we've got going on at work right now. So go on. Get out there and bring this guy in already."

If O'Malley hadn't been behind them studying his whiteboard, she would have kissed Ramirez in that moment.

"I'm serious," Avery said. "Call me to let me know what you find. If it's nothing, I want you by my side the rest of the way."

"I will," he replied, giving her a smile that communicated volumes. It let her know that he had forgiven her and that he still cared for her. He let her know that he would love to be by her side no matter what.

It also let her know that he had full confidence in her—that she would end up finding this creep and dragging him in.

And it was that last bit that set her down the hall, walking at a near-sprint, more determined than ever to catch this killer before he could claim another victim.

CHAPTER THIRTY FOUR

The information Duggan gave her was brief yet precise. It made her realize that even though the involvement of the bureau seemed tedious and almost invasive, they knew how to boil things down to the details. It made her wonder if she would have ever been able to cut it as an agent.

The information he had sent her told her that Roosevelt Toms's roommate for six months and two weeks was named Jason Inge. He was thirty-nine and worked as a car detailer, specializing in custom wraps and paint designs. He lived in a quiet neighborhood about two miles outside of the Dorchester area. The arson charge Duggan had mentioned was actually two: one for burning a playground at the age of sixteen and another at the age of twenty-three when he and a friend had attempted to burn an abandoned bar to the ground, apparently just for the hell of it. Since 2005, there had been no charges against him. He actually seemed to be an upstanding citizen who had even donated money to the Boston PD at the end of every year since 2009.

Avery read through all of this again after she parked in front of Jason Inge's house. The arson charges obviously made him something of a suspect, but the rest of the material didn't make her feel like she had anything worthwhile here. Still, she did her duty and stepped out of the car. It was 5:37 in the afternoon and she hoped that would have given him enough time to get home, assuming that car detailing was a nine-to-five sort of job.

She walked up the sidewalk to the small two-story house. It seemed idyllic, with its red shutters, immaculately clean porch, and recently mown lawn. When she stepped up onto the porch steps, she almost felt like she was trespassing.

There was no doorbell, just an iron knocker on the front door. She lifted it and clanged it down, knocking three times. When no one had answered after thirty seconds, she knocked again. When she still got no answer, she assumed that Jason Inge was still at work. She looked back to the street and saw the truck that was parked almost directly in front of the house. She nearly called Ramirez to ask him to run a plate for her but figured she could do some scouting herself before she bothered anyone else.

She left the porch and walked back down the sidewalk. She checked the truck—a small-bodied Toyota—and found it locked. There was nothing incriminating to be found from a simple glance through the passenger window. She turned back to the house and eyed its small yard. A stretch of grass on the right of the house led to a backyard while a picket fence separated the left side yard from the neighbor.

She walked to the right and along the edge of the house. As she did, she listened for any signs of talking, music, or a television making its racket. But she heard nothing other than her own quiet footfalls in the grass. When she reached the back of the house, it was more of the same: a clean and crisp yard, a small back porch with a grill, and a set of concrete stairs on the far right edge of the house that she assumed led into a basement.

Even the mere thought of a basement reminded her of Phillip Bailey and with that, she was not able to ignore the house simply because it appeared that no one was home. She walked toward the basement stairs and along the way, noticed the green city trash bin tucked directly beside the far edge of the patio. A blue city-issued recycle bin sat beside it.

With a scowl, Avery popped open the top to the green can. A white garbage bag was on top, sitting on top of an identical bag. There were small bits of trash tucked between the two: junk mail, a milk carton, and—

Her eyes stopped at the milk carton. There was a film of dust on it that looked very much like ash. The same gray residue was also on the white trash bag on the bottom of the bin. She reached it and removed the top bag.

The sight of the small bones that trickled down the side of the bin nearly made her jump back. There, mingled in with what was unmistakably ash, were the bones of some sort of animal. Further down she saw the rear of some other animal. Its hide was scorched almost down to the bone but its long tail made it clear that it was a cat.

She also saw a shirt down there. It was crumpled and balled up, but she could see that it was a light pink in color. What she could see of the collar indicated that it was low-cut—and almost definitely not a man's shirt.

Concerned now, she went ahead and tipped the garbage bin over. When she did, a cloud of dust came wafting out. But she knew better. It was not dust. It was ash. As it drifted by her pants, she took a step backward. She went down to a knee and peered into the bottom of the bin.

There was more ash at the bottom—a pile of it, in fact.

She looked back up to the back porch with wide eyes, almost expecting someone to be there. But the porch was empty. She was alone.

She peered back into the garbage bin, looking at all of that ash.

The shirt had also moved. Avery could clearly see that it was a woman's shirt. And it was torn down the back from the collar.

Her heart pounded.

This was not his roommate's address.

It was *his* address.

An alias.

And here she was, alone.

With a surprisingly steady hand, she grabbed her phone. She pulled up Ramirez's number as if by instinct and brought the phone to her ear.

He answered on the first ring. Hearing his calm confidence eased her a bit. "Hey," he said. "What's up?"

"I'm at Jason Inge's residence. No one is answering the door but there's a truck parked directly in front of the house. I peeked in a garbage bin around back. I've got a series of small bones, what looks like a partially burned cat, a huge amount of ash and what looks like a woman's shirt. Now that I'm closer to it, I think I also smell something…butane…lighter fluid or something like that."

"For real?"

"Yes. I think it might be—"

A sound to her right interrupted her. It was a scream…a high-pitched scream that was greatly muffled. She couldn't be absolutely sure, but she thought it had come from the direction of the basement steps.

"You still there?" Ramirez asked.

"Yeah. I think I just heard a scream from inside. Get over here as quick as you can. Maybe bring some backup."

"I'm on it. Please be safe."

"You know me," she said, and killed the call.

She drew her sidearm and slowly started for the basement stairs.

That's when she heard the noise again, louder this time and more panicked.

Avery's slow stride turned into a run as she reached the basement stairs and headed own toward the basement doors where the screaming continued, growing more urgent with every second.

CHAPTER THIRTY FIVE

The basement door was locked, which was not much of a surprise. Avery didn't even bother throwing a shoulder into it or trying to kick it in; if she failed, she'd be alerting the killer to her presence and she knew that the element of surprise might be the only advantage she had here. She hurried back up the concrete steps and into the backyard. She then made her way to the back porch, making sure to step carefully but quickly.

That door was also locked but a square of paned glass sat along the top of it so those inside could look out into the backyard. Avery drew her arm back, made a V-shape out of her elbow, and shoved it hard into the glass. The shattering glass and subsequent tinkling as shards fell to the floor inside wasn't too loud; hopefully they had gone unheard by anyone in the basement.

Avery reached her hand carefully into the broken window. She had to get up on her tiptoes to get hand low enough inside to find the doorknob. Her fingers found it and she turned the lock counterclockwise, careful not to cut herself on the fragments of glass that remained in the pane. With the door unlocked, she opened it and stepped inside and withdrew her sidearm, a Glock 0.9mm that was starting to feel like an extension of herself.

She found herself inside a small kitchen. A few dirty dishes were in the sink and the small kitchen table was littered with mail and random papers. Avery ignored this, moving further into the house. As she stepped out of the kitchen and into the adjoining living room, she heard another scream to her right, unmistakably below her.

Off of the living room, there was a small hallway that made up the rest of the house. She checked each room as she passed, as the doors were all standing open. There were two bedrooms, one bathroom, and a linen closet. That left one door remaining at the far end of the hall. This door was closed. As she approached it, she heard muffled whimpers from behind it, faint and almost non-existent.

If this door was locked, she'd have to try breaking it down. She may even need to blow the knob and lock off with her Glock, giving herself away if there was someone down below. She reached out and turned the knob. She relaxed instantly when it turned under her hand.

She pushed the door open and a set of wooden stairs was revealed. She took the first step down, testing the strength of it to see of it would creak under her weight. Confident that it was sturdy and would not give her away, she took a second stair down.

Beneath her, another of those whimpering noises sounded out. This time, Avery was able to hear another voice with it. It was a male voice, but soft and somber.

"The pain is momentary, I think," he was saying. "It will be much better if you just accept it. It will be over before you know it."

"Why?" the woman asked, her voice nothing more than a tremor.

"I don't think you'd understand," the man said.

This was followed by the sound of a loud clunking noise that was almost hydraulic in nature. The woman cried out loudly in a brief yelp.

Avery took two more steps down—there were ten more to go. She saw that near the bottom, there was open space between each stair, revealing the basement area below. If the killer saw her feet before she could gauge the situation, she could lose her advantage.

She took a deep breath and bounded down the stairs as quickly as she could. As she did, the woman let out a scream and there were the sounds of a struggle. The woman was crying out now, letting out loud wails of horror.

Avery reached the bottom of the stairs and when her feet hit the concrete, everything seemed to happen in a sped-up sort frenzy, like someone had pressed a fast-forward button.

Avery took a single moment to take in the scene. The sheer absurdity of it made her hesitate for just a moment.

The man had heard her and wheeled around to face her. They were in a small basement area occupied with only a small work desk along the right side of the room. But behind the man she saw a strange-looking door that almost resembled a heavy-duty door to an industrial icebox or cooler. A woman was inside of it, having been knocked down and getting to her feet. All around her, flames were licking upward and growing with unreal quickness.

Avery trained her gun on the man and took three huge strides forward. She took a good look at the man's face. She recalled the picture Agent Lewis had showed on the Skype call.

I'm right, this is Roosevelt Toms, she thought. *Toms has been living under the alias of Jason Inge.*

"Don't move," Avery said. "Drop to the ground and—"

Toms didn't let her finish before he wheeled around and slammed the industrial-type door shut. It made that same hydraulic-like sound Avery had heard. Inside, the woman screamed but the sound was cut off as the door was slammed closed. Toms then grabbed a large plank and worked quickly to work it through a set of handles that would barricade the door if the person inside *did* manage to escape.

Avery rushed forward and shoved Toms hard against the wall. He collided hard, the back of his head striking the concrete wall, and let out a cry as he sank to the floor. The plank he had tried to use to barricade the door clattered to the floor. Avery wasted no time, placing her hands on the U-shaped handle of the heavy door. With a grunt, she pulled it open.

An intense wave of heat rushed out at her. She took a step back away from it and as she did, the woman inside came barreling out. She was screaming and flailing wildly with a trail of flame behind her. Avery could smell burning clothes and hair.

The woman ran directly into Avery and they both went to the floor in a heap of arms and legs. Avery's right arm twisted beneath her and hit the floor hard, sending her gun sliding across the floor and a bolt of electric pain up toward her shoulder.

She rolled away from the burning woman, feeling the flames now licking at the leg of her pants. With a hard shove that was probably a little too forceful, Avery sent the woman careening hard to the right. She was still screaming, rolling around and trying to put the flames out. Avery, meanwhile, scrambled for her gun while keeping her eyes on Roosevelt Toms.

He was getting to his feet and taking in the sight before him. Beside him, the flames inside his torturous little room continued to grow. They were burning furiously, flashing out of the door on occasion. The roaring noise the fire made as it grew and consumed whatever fuel he had in the room was monstrous.

Avery grabbed her gun and looked around the room for something that might help put out the flames that were still scorching the woman on the floor. She wondered then if this was Sophia Lesbrook who was burning—who was even now giving off the smell of charred flesh.

There's nothing here, Avery thought. *Nothing to put these flames out.*

Sophia continued to scream and roll, now in a spastic sort of way that reminded Avery of a broken remote-controlled toy. Thinking as quickly as she could, Avery tore off the button-down shirt she was wearing, revealing the thin tank top beneath. The buttons flew in all directions but the plinking noises they made as they hit the floor were drowned out by the roaring of the fire from inside the small room.

151

She went to Sophia Lesbrook and threw the shirt on her, trying her best to flatten it against the flames. She did this several times, almost in a fanning motion. It seemed to bring the flames down a bit but Avery felt her own hands burning as she fought the fire that was slowly dying out on Sophia's bare arms and her right leg.

She also continued to keep a check on Toms. He was on his feet now but clearly dazed from the whack he'd taken to the head.

"Don't you *dare* move," Avery yelled at him. "Stay where you are."

He blinked rapidly, trying to clear the cobwebs from his head. As she watched him, her right arm grew hot and she realized that the one remaining flame on Sophia had licked upward and burned her arm. She drew back with a hiss and when she did, Roosevelt Toms came rushing at her.

Avery drew her Glock up and fired a shot just as Toms threw his shoulder into her ribs. Toms roared out in pain and Avery was able to shove him off of her before finding herself on the floor again. She stalked over to him and saw that her shot had taken him high in the right shoulder. He was on the floor, trying to get up without using his right arm.

Avery kicked him in the ribs and then pushed him over with her foot. When he was on his back and facing her, she saw that he held something in his hands. She saw it a split second too late, though.

It was a yellow tin can of something. Before she could figure out what it was, he was spraying something into her face. The smell as it hit her face was intense and thick.

Lighter fluid...

This idea flashed through her mind as she stumbled back. The liquid had partly gotten into her eyes and it was stinging like mad as she tried to shake it away. She wiped at her eyes but that seemed to only make it worse. The world was a blur and she could barely even make out any shapes or colors.

That's when she felt Toms kick her right knee. She felt it buckle but was pretty sure nothing had popped out of place. Still, she went to the floor on one knee. She held her gun out although she could see nothing, hoping it might intimidate Toms.

Instead, she felt a hard pulling sensation at her scalp as he grabbed her hair in his hands. She felt a hard kick to her stomach and the wind went rushing out of her. He then started to grapple with her for the possession of her gun. Even though she could not see, she knew she could not let him have the Glock. If he got it, the

152

fight was over—her life might very well be over, either by gunshot or by being thrown into his makeshift furnace.

She staggered to her feet, keeping in mind that he had a bum right shoulder from the first shot. So if she kept her pressure to the right and focused her strength there, she should be able to overtake him easily. As they fought for the gun, she continued to hear Sophia Lesbrook screaming from the floor. She also felt an intense heat behind her and tried to recall the exact position of the door along the wall. If he fought her backward too much, he could easily shove her into his little furnace.

Instead, she felt him pushing her to the left, where she collided with the wall. Her eyes were stinging and her stomach was aching but she'd be damned if she'd give up. She fought against him hard, feeling the gun still in her hands as he tried to tear it away. She tried to get a better idea of where his hands were along the gun. Taking a chance, she angled it to the right, feeling his weakness to that side.

With a cry of desperation, Avery pulled the trigger. For a brief moment, she felt him release the gun. She opened her eyes as wide as she could, only seeing blurs. She saw one directly in front of her and fired. But the blur kept coming at her. It went low and she tried firing again but was struck along the waist. Again, she was slammed against the wall but this time she did not give Toms time to get a good position on her. She pushed back, driving him backward by pushing his weight to the right, where he was unable to fight back. She felt him trying to trip her and they fought while moving across the room, the fire still roaring around them.

Two more seconds of this and they came to an abrupt stop. They had hit the small desk she had spied when taking in the room. They fought against it and something fell to the ground in a clatter of noise. Again, she smelled that chemical smell that might be butane or propane.

"You're going to burn, bitch," Toms hissed

Stupid, she thought.

By speaking to her, she was able to locate exactly where he was standing. He had nearly whispered the comment into her right ear, meaning that he was leaning in that direction. With a surge of strength, she drew her hand (and, at the same time, his own as he continued to fight for purchase of the gun) and fired twice.

She felt him release the gun right away. She then heard him thump against the desk and then the floor.

Unable to see him, she had no idea if he was dead or not. The only things she was certain of was that Sophia Lesbrook was whimpering somewhere nearby and that the room was growing hotter. Not knowing what else to do, Avery spit on her fingers and wiped at her eyes, hoping that any sort of moisture might clear her vision. It helped, but not much. The sting was still there and although she could now see more than just a blur, things were still very hazy.

"Sophia Lesbrook?" she asked.

"Unnh," was the only response she got.

"Are you still on fire?"

"No." Her voice was shaky and faint, like a frightened child.

"Is the man dead?"

There was silence for a moment. In that silence, Avery felt her way along the desk she and Toms had collided into. She was trying to find her way back to the stairs but was very disoriented due to the near-blindness and the heat.

"I think so," Sophia said. "But the fire...it's out of that room. Something fell...off the desk when you were fighting. The fire came out of the door and caught it. It's in here with us now."

Shit, Avery thought. *Hopefully the concrete floor will slow it enough for me to figure something out.*

"Sophia, can you walk? How badly are you burned?"

"I don't know...I—" And then she started crying.

I have to clean my eyes, Avery thought. *If I don't get out of here soon, I'll be burned alive. Both of us will be.*

That's when she started to smell something burning. Something like wood. And the smell of whatever chemical had been sprayed into her face was stronger than ever. "Sophia, do you—"

But her question was cut off by an enormous sound that was almost like wind. It was accompanied by a tremendous heat that was so fast and intense, it knocked Avery to the floor. In a single moment, it felt like every hair on her arms was singed.

Sophia Lesbrook started to scream again. She was trying to speak but it was coming out in nothing but a frantic jumble. Still, Avery was pretty sure she knew what had happened. Sophia had told her the fire had come out of that room and lit something aflame within the basement. Apparently, that fire had touched the same chemical that had been sprayed in her face—perhaps something that had been spilled from the desk.

Okay, okay, she thought, getting back to her feet. *I can do this. I'll fall on my ass a few times but I can get Sophia to the stairs and—*

"He's not dead!"

It was Sophia's voice, nearly hysterical now. "I was wrong! He's—"

But her voice was quickly cut off.

Still blinded and now almost dizzy with heat and the knowledge that she could be burned alive at any moment, Avery held her gun in front of her as she took slow steps backward. Smoke filled the air and stung her nostrils. For a moment, she thought this might be what hell was like.

That notion only intensified when she felt the first of the growing flames lap at her leg, burning her pants and touching the flesh beneath it.

CHAPTER THIRTY SIX

Avery had seen how quickly the fire had grown in that little makeshift furnace. She figured if it also grew that quickly outside of the room, she might have thirty seconds to get upstairs before she went up in flames. She might be able to do it even while blinded…but she was not going to leave Sophia behind.

More than that, if Toms was still alive, that made things even harder. Knowing it was useless to stand in place—especially with a flame actively eating away at her pants leg—Avery stepped forward, in the direction she was pretty sure Sophia was in. Fortunately, it was the same direction she needed to go to escape the growing fire behind her.

"Sophia, can you come to me?"

"No. He's—"

Avery started feeling out with her feet for Sophia's body while still holding out her Glock. She was starting to smell smoke that seemed to get thicker by the second.

"Sophia, I need you to get to the stairs. When you get there, start calling me. I can't see and I—"

She was interrupted by a hard punch to the face. She heard a muffled cry behind it—a cry of pain and of triumph.

How's this asshole still alive? she wondered. Her jaw ached fiercely but she'd been punched enough to know that he had not been able to put his full power into it.

She caught herself against the desk and when she did, the heat against her arm and back was immense. She yelled out and tried angling to the left but another punch caught her, this time to her stomach.

She doubled over, gasping slightly and then coughing from the sudden intake of smoke. As she bent over, she fired off another shot. As she did this, she surged forward, having no idea if she had hit Toms with the round or not.

She was then struck from behind. She went hard to the floor and again lost her grip on her gun.

"Get to the stairs, Sophia!"

It was hard to breathe because of the blow to her stomach and because of the smoke that was filling the room and her lungs. She was given one blessing, though; her eyes were clearing up a bit. She could now see Sophia Lesbrook, hobbling toward the stairs through a cloud of smoke and glowing flames. Behind her, back toward the door, fire had crept out of the furnace room and engulfed a stack of papers that had fallen from the desk as well as the desk itself. The flames were tall and starving, reaching up and brushing against the ceiling. She also saw a crumpled and melting bucket among the debris. She wondered if it had contained a chemical that had caused the sudden intensity of the fire that had knocked her down.

She felt something odd at her back as Roosevelt Toms fell upon her. She felt like someone was pouring water on her and then realized with horror that she could smell the scent of propane or butane or whatever the hell it was again. Toms was dousing her in it.

"Let her escape," Toms said. "I don't care. You can take her place."

She rolled over hard and threw him off. When she did, she inhaled smoke far too quickly and started to cough again. The vision that she had just regained went hazy again as she scooted herself back, gagging on the smoke and wondering if she was going to suffocate or burn to death first.

My gun, she thought. *If he gets it before I do, maybe a shot to the head would be faster.*

As if birthed by that thought, the room was suddenly filled with gunshots.

Two of them.

Avery tensed up, waiting for the pain, sure that she was dead.

Three seconds passed before she realized that she was still breathing.

"Avery," a voice said. It was a voice that made her nearly start crying. She might have done just that if the smoke hadn't been strangling her.

It was Ramirez.

She felt his hands on her shoulder. "Can you get up?" he asked.

She nodded and got to her feet. She swayed a bit but steadied herself against him. "I can't see. He sprayed me with something...some sort of...ah God. Where's Sophia?"

"She's fine," Ramirez said as they made their way to the stairs. "I sent her running out the back door. The living room floor upstairs is already starting to buckle and burn. Come on...you reek of lighter fluid. Let's get you upstairs before it's too late."

She could barely see anything as Ramirez led her up the wooden stairs. She banged her shins a few times and almost fell down but Ramirez caught her. When they were up the stairs and into the hallway, she was able to take her first whole breath without the hazard of smoke.

She was half-dragged through the kitchen, where the back door was standing open. The fresh air was a blessing…like cool water in the desert.

"Wait," she said. "Water…for my eyes."

Ramirez quickly took her to the kitchen sink. As he helped her splash water into her eyes, Avery realized that she could hear the place burning. Boards were popping and the structure was creaking all around them. Slowly, the smell of smoke started to meet them in the kitchen.

As Ramirez gently helped her clean her eyes, the first thing she saw clearly was his face. Knowing that it was a foolish waste of time, she flung her arms around her him and kissed him. She again almost resorted to tears, which was unlike her. She managed to hold them back as they broke the kiss and hurried outside.

Avery collapsed on the grass in the backyard not too far away from Sophia. Ramirez sat beside her in the grass and she listened as he called the fire department to report the fire and then called O'Malley.

Avery was in and out, coughing one moment and feeling hazy the next. She was pretty sure she passed out somewhere between Ramirez looking over Sophia and hearing the first wail of sirens approaching them in the distance.

"You almost died," Ramirez said, looking down to her.

"I know," she said. "It all happened so fast and I lost control."

"I know. That's how you are. But you're alive. That's the important thing."

Avery nodded and looked over to Sophia. Her eyes were open, looking up the darkening evening sky. She reached out and took Sophia's hand.

"How are you doing?"

Sophia tried to speak but only cried.

It was the only sound in the yard until the first of several fire trucks pulled up three minutes later.

CHAPTER THIRTY SEVEN

Avery sat at the table, O'Malley and Connelly on the other side facing her. Nothing much had happened in the two weeks that had passed ever since she'd made it out of Roosevelt Toms's house. In fact, the only thing that felt different to Avery was the sore and discolored scar on her leg. She'd managed to come out of the inferno with nothing more than a second-degree burn and fatigue brought on by smoke inhalation.

Outside of that, most everything was the same. That included the decision that O'Malley had given her to make sixteen days ago.

She tried to focus, to push the flashbacks of the flames out of her head.

A promotion, she thought. *I like what I do now. If I take the sergeant position, I'll have to deal with more politics. But the respect...the sense of accomplishment...*

"Avery?"

It was Connelly. Every now and then when he was at his most sincere, he would call her by her first name. Never O'Malley, though.

"Yes?"

"This is your decision," he said. "You will not be looked down upon if you choose not to take it. And if you *do* take it, it would take effect at the end of next week."

"That's right," O'Malley said.

Avery shrugged. "I just don't know. It seems...too unexpected, I guess."

O'Malley sighed and leaned forward. "This isn't about what happened in that house, is it?"

"What do you mean?" she asked.

"You almost died," he said. "If Ramirez had been ten or twenty seconds later, you would have died. I've been there before. It scares the shit out of you. And there's no shame in that."

"No. It's not that."

O'Malley nodded. "So...is this a no?"

Avery gave a thin grin. Under the desk, her burn scar itched. "Is this a one-time offer?" she asked.

O'Malley and Connelly exchanged a look and shrugged at one another. "Honestly, probably not," O'Malley said.

"Then it's a no for now."

Both men nodded in unison. She was pretty sure they had been expecting it. O'Malley drummed his hands on the table and then

159

cleared his throat. "Connelly, let me talk to Black in private, would you?"

Connelly took his leave without a word and closed the door behind him. For a moment, O'Malley studied her with great interest.

"Have you gone to see Sloane Miller since you came back to work last week?" he asked.

"No."

"Do you think you should?"

Honestly, she had no idea. It seemed silly, but she also knew the severity of the situation she had been in. Looking back on it was like hell itself, really.

"And is Sophia Lesbrook still texting you?"

"I haven't gotten a text from her in three days. I think she finally wants to put it all behind her."

Sophia had texted Avery almost continuously during the first week. Avery was pretty sure it was probably Sophia's way of trying to rationalize what had happened to her. Sophia had not been as fortunate as Avery; when all was said and done, she'd suffered three third-degree burns on her right arm, one on her back, and a second-degree burn on her scalp. She had been overly thankful during those first few days and had texted Avery as if they had been lifelong friends who had endured a trauma together.

"You okay?" O'Malley asked.

"Yeah," she said, blinking the thoughts away.

But really, she was scared. She'd almost died. And it was hard to accept.

Avery felt the scar still itching under the table. The scar scared her, too.

And so did Ramirez.

She'd tried denying it all week long but she was becoming fairly certain that she was falling in love with him. If she'd needed one final thing to drive it home after all of their time together, it had been the surge of relief and utter trust that had swept through her when she'd heard him speak her name in that smoky cellar when she had been blinded.

She felt the need to tell him but knew it would be a bad idea. It would change not only their personal relationship drastically (perhaps, she thought, even *end* it) and would wreck their working relationship.

Thinking of him, she suddenly did not want to be in the conference room with O'Malley. She stood up and looked thoughtfully down at O'Malley.

160

"I appreciate the opportunity you've given me, but I'm not ready for it yet. But thanks for the trust and the respect."

"You've earned it," O'Malley said. "Now get out of here. I'll check in on you tomorrow. And I hope you'll make an appointment with Sloane."

"I will," she said as she headed for the door, walking on a leg that she was starting to think might itch for the remainder of her life.

***

One thing she'd learned while in the hospital was that her first reaction had been correct: the man in the house had been Roosevelt Toms. He had been living under the alias of an old roommate, Jason Inge, for about eleven months—apparently around the time he had started to prepare himself for the killings.

He'd died from Ramirez's gunshots. One to the center of the head, the other a bit higher. He'd also been shot two other times by Avery's gun, once in the shoulder and once in the thigh. His body had been pulled from the wreckage after the fire department had extinguished the fire. He'd been very badly burned but not nearly as badly as the people he had killed.

Avery hated that she thought of Roosevelt Toms whenever she saw Ramirez now. It was currently happening as they sat in her apartment and had dinner. Ramirez had brought Chinese takeout. They had plans for an intimate night later on, but she wasn't sure it was going to happen.

Yes, he was scaring her, too. She didn't know if she had the energy to love someone right now. But God, it was nice to be around him.

What's a girl to do?

"What are you thinking about?" he asked her over their Moo Shoo Pork.

"Roosevelt Toms," she admitted.

"You've got to stop that," he said.

"I know. But I can't help it. I almost died and you had to kill him. I mean, he was…he was a—"

"He was a man with a very unfortunate history. We've been through this. His father died and was cremated when Toms was young. Toms resented his mother for it, especially when she made him scatter his ashes. I can recite it over and over again, Avery. I can even recall the grandmother that spoke to us and gave us the information."

161

She smiled at him, appreciating how well he knew her. He was running through the bio they had compiled on Toms because he knew it would take logic and the repeating of information to finally get her unstuck from thoughts of Roosevelt Toms.

"Thanks for sticking with me through this," she said. "I know it's a lot. And I know that I haven't always treated you the way you *should* be treated."

"Avery?"

"Yes?"

"I care a lot about you. And unless I hear it from your lips that you don't want anything to do with me, I'll always be here for you. However you need me. That's a promise."

Yeah, I'm falling in love with him.

She reached out and took his hand. "Thank you," she said, looking into his eyes. She thought the night might end up in the bedroom after all and—

Her cell phone chirped from the living room as a text message came in.

"One second," she said. She got up from the table and retrieved her phone. Her heart soared a bit when she read the name above the text display.

Rose.

Beneath it was a simple message that made Avery wonder what she had done to deserve the good fortune that seemed to have stuck with her after coming out of Toms's house. The potential promotion (which she had turned down), Ramirez sticking by her side, and now this.

The text message read:

I figured it's time to see you somewhere other than the hospital. Sorry I've been a bitch. I'm lonely and bored and Marcus-less tonight. Wondering if I could come over for wine and a cheesy movie.

While she was pretty sure she was falling in love with Ramirez, it wasn't even a close call. She took her cell phone to Ramirez and showed it to him. He chuckled when he was done reading it, wiped his mouth with a napkin, and stood up. As he started to box up his remaining food, he said, "Say no more. Girls' night. I get it."

"Do you?" Avery asked.

"Yeah. I know how much you want things right with her. I know it's been killing you that she hasn't reached out since she came by the hospital to see you. Have fun."

He means it, she thought.

She smiled back at him and covered the few feet between them. She cupped her hand to the back of his neck and kissed him hard. Within seconds, the fierceness of it dissolved into something softer, something more passionate. When it broke, they were looking into each other's eyes.

And she saw that he was scared, too.

COMING SOON!

Book #4 in the Avery Black mystery series!

Blake Pierce

Blake Pierce is author of the bestselling RILEY PAGE mystery series, which includes seven books (and counting). Blake Pierce is also the author of the MACKENZIE WHITE mystery series, comprising four books (and counting); of the AVERY BLACK mystery series, comprising four books (and counting); and of the new KERI LOCKE mystery series.

An avid reader and lifelong fan of the mystery and thriller genres, Blake loves to hear from you, so please feel free to visit www.blakepierceauthor.com to learn more and stay in touch.

BOOKS BY BLAKE PIERCE

RILEY PAIGE MYSTERY SERIES
ONCE GONE (Book #1)
ONCE TAKEN (Book #2)
ONCE CRAVED (Book #3)
ONCE LURED (Book #4)
ONCE HUNTED (Book #5)
ONCE PINED (Book #6)
ONCE FORSAKEN (Book #7)

MACKENZIE WHITE MYSTERY SERIES
BEFORE HE KILLS (Book #1)
BEFORE HE SEES (Book #2)
BEFORE HE COVETS (Book #3)
BEFORE HE TAKES (Book #4)

AVERY BLACK MYSTERY SERIES
CAUSE TO KILL (Book #1)
CAUSE TO RUN (Book #2)
CAUSE TO HIDE (Book #3)
CAUSE TO FEAR (Book #4)

KERI LOCKE MYSTERY SERIES
A TRACE OF DEATH (Book #1)
A TRACE OF MURDER (Book #2)

Made in the USA
Monee, IL
29 January 2022

90251787R00100